Life's Twists and Turns

A Collection of Stories

By Starla Criser

Starla

ENTERPRISES, INC.

For information regarding permission, write to Starla Enterprises, Inc.

Attention: Permissions Department,

9415 E. Harry St., Ste. 603, Wichita, KS 67207

First Edition

ISBN: 978-0-578-40995-5

Text copyright © 2019 by Starla Criser

Cover copyright © 2019 by Angela Criser

Published by Starla Enterprises, Inc.

DEDICATION

This fictional story collection could not have been written without the support of many people who have passed through my life.

My father-in-law, Max Criser, was a much appreciated and treasured reader of many of my stories. He supported me in so many ways and will be in my heart and memories forever.

My much-missed parents, Opal M. (Wahl) and Jack L. Tolliver, supported me in everything I did in my early years. They gave me a lasting sense of love within a family. They guided me to honor the Golden Rule in how I deal with others around me.

My husband Steve has supported and loved me for over forty-eight years. He has been my rock, my confidante, and the person I most respect in my life.

My daughter Angela has supported me in so many ways, too. We are good friends and occasional traveling companions. She is always there to help me out of the problems I get into with anything from the computer to my phone. She is my best Beta reader and offers good suggestions, as well as excellent help with the whole publishing process.

My good friend Cherise Langenberg has supported me in countless ways as well. She is one of the most kind-hearted people I know. Her work situation can be trying at times, but she faces it with the strength of her faith in God and in people. She listens to anyone needing a concerned ear and caring heart. She can laugh at life, enjoy her family and friends, and cry with someone when they suffer a low time in their life.

ABOUT

She tries to live every day as the gift it is. Facing life's problems and staying strong, remembering to laugh, and holding family and friends close to her heart are important to Starla. She feels fortunate to have a good support system around her. Loyal friends, caring people she works with in the community, her family, and especially her husband and daughter give her strength and encouragement.

As a long-time writer she has written in many genres, under other names. Her recent writing focus is on children's books in two different series. Her Blossom the cow series features an imaginative cow and her animal friends. The Lucy the hedgehog series centers on the adventures of Lucy and her guinea pig friend Sophia.

Working in her community with some wonderful older adults interested in writing, Starla has expanded her writing to stories about older relationships. Her previous story collection, Timeless Love, was her first attempt in this area. This larger story collection, Life's Twists and Turns, continues with reflections on how we adapt to the many changes in our lives as we age.

Website: starlacriser.com

TABLE OF CONTENTS

THE MAGIC OF A CINNAMON ROLL

"Seriously?" As Bernie rushed back into the kitchen, he wrinkled his nose at the smell of over-cooked spaghetti. Steam wafted up from the pan in which the water had nearly boiled away. "I only stepped away for a couple minutes," he complained in disgust.

His oldest daughter had called and his cell phone was in the living room. Not that he blamed her for his latest cooking disaster. He'd been sure this time he had mastered making simple pasta. He'd read the directions on the box. Twice. However, failing to lower the heat on the burner before he'd left the room was a big no-no. Now a big ball of dough sat in a clump at the bottom of the pan.

He flicked off the burner, disappointed again. It wearied him having one cooking calamity after another. For a seventy-four-year-old man with two complicated degrees and who had worked for more than fifty years before retiring, he should be able to make a decent meal.

His stomach rumbled. His pantry was fully stocked and he could try again. But he wasn't in the mood to try his hand at ruining anything else tonight. "Guess I'll be dining out. Again."

He blinked. When had he started talking to himself?

It unnerved him. I need to get out and socialize more. Well, going out to eat would satisfy his current need for palatable food and for socialization. A temporary solution to both matters.

The gooey glob caught his attention and he frowned in annoyance. He carried the pan to the sink, used the spatula to scrape out most of the lump, then filled it with water. The mess could sit there until he returned home and was ready to deal with getting rid of the evidence of his inability to cook.

He missed Harriet for so many reasons. Not the least being her skills in the kitchen. She'd died a year ago and her much used, stained apron continued hanging in the pantry. Her box of recipes remained on the corner of the cabinet by the microwave. He'd stopped trying to make sense of them. With his lifelong love of research, he'd discovered a big selection of cooking magazines at the bookstore. He now had subscriptions to three. Not that any of them had done him the least bit of good but he refused to give up. He needed a better plan for learning to cook.

No point in lollygagging in here, he was hungry. Tired, too. He still had trouble sleeping in the bed that felt big and empty. Every day he awakened in less pain about not having the love of his life waking beside him. He would take back every groused comment about Harriet hogging the sheets or warming her cold feet against his legs to have her with him again.

He wiped his hands with a hand towel, jutted out his chin, straightened his shoulders, and headed out of the kitchen. Put him in front of a high-tech computer with a bunch of other programmers and he was in his element. A kitchen was a world with many mysteries.

As he walked into the living room that looked the same as it always had, he glanced at his favorite leather recliner with the many worn spots. It had needed reupholstering for a long time but he didn't care. The chair fit him and that was all that mattered. He thought about the numerous times he saw something interesting on the news and still turned toward Harriet's chair next to his, ready to share the tidbit with her. Would he ever stop doing that?

His eyes misted and he felt the sting of tears. His heart pinched at thinking about the great loss in his life. He would get past this moment of loneliness, he always did. Not that he would ever forget his dear wife. Although he had days when the TV or a good book kept him here, he didn't just sit at home. The bookstore drew him, even the computer store in the mall with its rows of the latest in electronics lured him out. But they weren't "social" trips where he mixed with others. His son and daughter kept telling him to join a book club, take an exercise class with other people his age, or visit a senior center. Even Harriet whispered to him sometimes in his dreams about meeting new people.

Lately, his kids had joined forces, trying to convince him to sell the house. "It's too big for you." "There are some nice senior apartment complexes." He hated those ideas, and, so far, Harriet hadn't whispered to encourage him to make such a change. He shoved that irritating subject aside.

It had been a week since he'd gone to Maggie's Place, an old-fashioned sixties-style diner he'd frequented more and more. Just considering going there made his stomach growl. He hoped the sweet-tempered Maggie would be there. Maybe she would even stop by his table to share a piece of her remarkable apple pie with him. Even better would be one of her amazing cinnamon rolls. His mood lightened at remembering her friendly smile, the twinkle in her gentle blue eyes as she teased him about his cooking failures.

******

There were dozens of restaurants in Wichita, Kansas, many wonderful choices for people who enjoyed eating out. It always amazed and pleased Maggie Carter that her small diner stayed packed nearly every night. She'd celebrated her sixty-eighth birthday last week. All too often these days, there seemed to be one new minor health issue or another develop. Her body warned her she needed to consider retiring. Her grown children thought she should sell the business, or at least cut back on the hours she spent here. But she'd told them this was her life. Her home. It had been this way since she and her husband had opened it forty-three years ago. At the time, she had told him they should call it Zach's Place but he insisted naming it after her, saying, "Everything good in my life starts with you, Maggie."

She stood in the kitchen doorway, satisfied. The smell of onions frying in butter for burgers, the juicy scent of their special meatloaf, and the yeasty rolls fresh out of the oven wafted around her. Some of her patrons teased her that they gained five pounds just inhaling the smells.

She looked at the filled seats in the dining room. Mr. and Mrs. Peters were in their regular booth, studying the menu, as if they didn't have it memorized after being here every week for almost ten years. Sandra Fowler sat in her normal booth at the back with her twin boys. Teenagers now. When had that happened? She'd brought them here since the boys could toddle into the diner.

Everywhere Maggie looked, she saw people she knew so well. They weren't just customers, they were friends. She talked with them and shared in their lives. The Peters both had heart issues that worried them. Sandra had started back to college, having long wanted to finish her nursing degree. Many of her other regulars shared things, too. And she shared back. They asked after her son and his family or about her daughter struggling with a recent divorce. They gave honest opinions when she tried new recipes. And she enjoyed meeting new customers to get to know and feed.

She sighed, a headache pulsing as she worried about an unexpected problem. Her favorite part-time worker—sometime wait staff, sometime short-order cook—had given her his notice earlier today. He'd decided to move back to his hometown in North Carolina. She wished him well but it left her with a need to look for a replacement and fast.

The bell over the front door jingled drawing her back to the moment. She glanced at the enormous rooster clock behind the long Formica counter with its dozen red-vinyl-covered bar stools, which were all full tonight. She didn't have to look toward the door to know who had walked into her diner. Bernie Hayfield. Must have burned his supper again. She smiled to herself, thinking she should feel sorry for him but she didn't. Because it brought him here.

Maggie smiled with her usual happiness at seeing him. She watched the handsome rascal head for the last booth. A familiar warmth filled her as it did when he came around. After his beloved wife had died last year, he'd started coming here. He'd been grieving then, starving, too. His wife of fifty-three years had handled all the cooking and most of the household chores. He had discovered while he could help design a rocket to go into outer space, he couldn't figure out the mechanics of making a simple meal. Doing laundry had challenged him as well until his daughter had deigned to give him lessons. His kids kept trying to convince him to sell his house and move into one of those fancy senior places with housekeepers on staff and prepared meals. But he was resisting. Good for him.

Watching as the taller-than-average, still physically fit man slid into the vinyl-upholstered booth, Maggie remembered how she'd sat down with him that first time. He'd seemed so alone, so lost. She'd experienced those same feelings when her husband had passed on a dozen years earlier. Her heart had gone out to Bernie and she'd encouraged him to talk about Harriet. They'd eaten one of her special cinnamon rolls together. Actually, he'd had two that night. They'd shared a roll or slices of apple pie—his absolute favorite kind of pie—many times since then. In fact, the habit was affecting her waistline.

******

Bernie sensed Maggie coming closer and drew in the cinnamon scent that seemed to be her personal fragrance. It always made him hungry for one of her distinctive, enormous cinnamon rolls. This late there wouldn't be any left. He'd have to come in for breakfast tomorrow or, at least, one morning soon.

As she stopped next to his table, he prepared himself for her teasing, something he found he looked forward to. Too many people in his life still treated him with caution because of his recent widowhood. Even his kids acted that way. He'd grown tired of it. He wanted to laugh again, not take everything so seriously.

"What did you burn tonight?" Her blue eyes sparkled with mischief at her question.

He didn't take offense. "Spaghetti. Except I didn't burn it, more… I don't know… destroyed it." He chuckled, thinking about the mess he'd left in the sink. "I might even need to throw away the saucepan this time."

She giggled like a young girl and he found it charming. She had an engaging way about her that drew people to her small diner. No one stayed a stranger in her place. He couldn't remember the number of times he'd witnessed someone new wander in and within minutes she was visiting with them, making them feel welcome. Just as she'd done for him when he'd first come here. Harriet would have adored her. He didn't know why they hadn't come here. Well, yes, he did. Harriet had preferred to make their meals and he was more than happy to eat them.

He pushed away that memory. "What's the special tonight, Lady Maggie?" He smiled at the nickname he'd given her.

A blush crept up her lightly-wrinkled face at the endearment. He enjoyed the reaction. His feelings for this white-haired beauty had grown stronger. Maybe he should worry about that since his wife had not been gone long. Yet he knew Harriet would want him moving on with life. He would have wanted the same for her if the situation were reversed. She would always be in his heart, his first love. Just as he knew Zach would always be in Maggie's heart. He respected that.

Maggie leaned down and whispered, "Tell no one, but I saved you a cinnamon roll for your dessert." She straightened. "The special tonight is meatloaf and mashed potatoes."

She saved me a cinnamon roll. As if she'd sensed he would come in tonight after yet another cooking catastrophe. The idea both amused him and touched him.

"Dessert first?" He grinned. "Will you share it with me?"

Those expressive eyes warmed. "It's not right to eat dessert first, you know."

He shrugged. "So, will you? Share it with me?"

She beamed, bustled away, and was back sliding into the other side of the booth within a minute. She set the plate holding an immense cinnamon roll with thick icing that oozed over the sides between them, pushing a fork toward him.

"The first bite is mine!" She drove her fork into the gooey roll.

Bernie chortled. He was so glad he'd ruined that stupid spaghetti. What can I destroy tomorrow night?

The fork stopped halfway to her mouth and she appeared worried. Noticing his questioning look, she said, "Sorry," forcing a smile. "I've got a small problem here."

He perked up, eager to have something to find a solution for. It's what he'd done all his life: solved a computer programming issue at work or taken care of a repair at the house. "How can I help?"

"Pete just told me he is quitting this weekend. Moving away." She sighed. "I'm happy for him. Really." Her gaze met his, a twinkle in those pretty eyes. "Oh! Idea. Think you can take food orders? Clean off a table or two? Maybe do simple grilling?"

Surprised, he blinked, not knowing what to say. Was she being serious?

"Just kidding." She laughed at his startled expression. He didn't feel relieved, though.

"I know that stuff is way out of your comfort zone." She studied the chunk of the roll on her fork. "Unfortunately, I'm serious about needing to find a part-time staff person. Soon."

"Sorry to hear about your problem." He knew she put in too many hours here already. Her kids worried about her, he did, too. "I'm sure you'll find someone." He hoped so, anyway.

"It isn't as easy as you think." She looked sad for a moment, then her warm smile returned. "Enough about that. We've got this cinnamon roll to eat and conversation to share."

In between helping take and deliver other customers' orders, she sat with him as he ate the meatloaf and mashed potatoes. She even stole a bite of meatloaf from time to time, which he didn't mind at all. They talked about some of the latest happenings in town: a sports bar opening, the closing of a major department store, whether a new baseball stadium was needed. She kept the conversation light, not wanting to burden him with her troubles. But he could tell they worried her. And that worried him.

Finally, they'd devoured it all and he'd had enough coffee to keep him up half the night. She kept glancing around the busy diner. He saw her forehead pinching and she reached up to rub it. She had things to do, employee issues to deal with. She didn't need him hanging around.

"I'd better go." But he was reluctant to leave. "There's a book I want to finish." Not really.

Maggie appeared distracted, then regretful. "I've been a terrible companion tonight. I apologize." She slid out of the booth with a weak smile. "The next time you come in everything will be better. "

"Sure. No problem."

******

Bernie had tossed and turned all night. Maggie's worried expression had haunted him. He was the last person she needed help from. As she'd said, her world of running a diner was out of his comfort zone. Heck, he couldn't even handle his own kitchen.

He stood in front of his bathroom mirror, staring at the small nick on his face. His thoughts had wandered and he'd cut himself shaving. That hadn't happened in years. And his stomach roiled with nerves. He'd decided. He was about to do something crazy.

A half hour and at least a hundred repetitions of "What do you think you're doing?" Later he stopped in the doorway of Maggie's Place. It was seven o'clock. He pulled in a breath, glanced around at the few people who had come in for an early breakfast. His logical brain told him to retreat before anyone noticed him, particularly Maggie. His feet had stuck to the floor.

"What are you doing here so early?" The woman he had come to see but was now thinking of avoiding, gaped at him from behind the counter. She held a half-empty glass coffee pot inches above the hot plate where it belonged.

"I... uh," he stumbled over his explanation. At her raised eyebrow, he blurted out, "I came to apply for your job opening." Criminy, when had he ever been this unsure of himself?

She blinked in confusion. "What? Job opening?"

Heat crept up his face and under the collar of his button-front shirt. He'd debated for longer than necessary about whether to wear a Polo shirt, too casual, or one of his dress shirts from his work days, which made him more comfortable. Jeans? No, again too casual. Slacks? Maybe too formal. He'd settled on this shirt and khakis. Now he felt ridiculous about all that stewing over his outfit.

"I mean, if you haven't hired someone yet." He swallowed down a huge lump of nerves. "I'd like to apply for the job."

She blinked again, then a slow smile slid into place. As she set the coffee pot down, she faced him. "I haven't run an ad yet."

Sweat beaded his upper lip and under his arms. It seemed crazy hot for so early on this May morning. "I'm jumping the gun here, aren't I? I just... I just..." Wanted to help. Needed to be needed. This had seemed like a perfect solution to both matters, at two in the morning anyway.

Someone across the diner called out for a coffee refill. Maggie looked over, then grinned with her usual friendliness at the customer. "Be right there."

Bernie's feet had become unstuck and he turned toward the door. Time to go. He'd made a big enough of a fool out of himself. But, with clear lightning speed, Maggie was at his side, holding the coffee pot.

"How about we go take care of the customer together?" Nearly half a foot shorter, she looked up at him. Her eyes met his, filled with warmth and a secret understanding. "We can call it on-the-job training."

Bernie grinned, relaxing. "So, you don't think I'm an idiot for coming here? For offering to do a job I'm totally unqualified for?"

Pleasure danced in her gaze. "Not an 'idiot,' sweet." She laughed and he'd like to hear a lot more of it. "What will your kids think about Dad working for minimum wage at a diner? Far from the fancy, highly-paid work you retired from. It won't even use a wee bit of all that education you have."

He couldn't help laughing, too. She was right. His son and daughter would worry about him losing touch with reality and making irrational decisions. Except his reality was dealing with too much blasted loneliness daily. This little job ought to take care of it, nothing more rational than that. Plus, he'd get to spend a lot more time getting to know a woman who'd become special to him.

"Guess they'll have to deal with it." He trailed after Maggie as she moved across the dining space, weaving between tables. He liked the way she filled out the white waitress uniform she always wore. The apron was tied around her waist and its long tail hung down to her softly rounded...

What are you thinking? He shook himself from those surprising thoughts. But he couldn't deny that he liked her curvy, not ridiculous-model-thin body. Again, he corralled his thoughts. "So, I have the job?"

She glanced over her shoulder, giving him a sassy look. "We'll see how today goes. If you don't break too many dishes, don't scare away my customers, and don't burn too many things... Well, I suppose you've got yourself a new career."

NEVER FORGOTTEN

Lee's Aunt Mabel had been chatting up a storm ever since he'd picked her up at Rainbow Manor for Seniors. They had talked for months about this trip back to the farm where she'd been born and raised with four older brothers, all long dead. It had been his home, too. She had been like his second mother. He'd needed this loving woman in his life back then. Still did.

As she rehashed the latest Mexican Train Domino-playing incident with her friends, his mind wandered. At ninety-two, Mabel had outlived most of her family, including her husband and sister-in-law. His father, her younger brother, lived in Florida. Neither of them heard from him unless his father sent a card at Christmas and it only had his signature, no personal note. The relationship had been that way since his father abandoned him with Mabel when Lee's mother died at 33. Mabel had never had children of her own. She'd raised him from a broken-hearted boy of eight years.

He drew in a deep breath. He didn't want to dwell on his bitter feelings about the abandonment. What good did it do, anyway? Besides, he'd had other losses in his life, each one taking a piece of his heart.

Ten years ago, his precious wife Linda and their granddaughter Susanna had died in a senseless car crash caused by a drunk driver. He would never get over that loss. How could he? But he and his son's family had learned to adjust. Not forget but accept what couldn't be changed. Linda and Susanna had cherished his aunt as much as he did. She'd helped him get through the tragedy. At least the driver had gone to jail for his act of careless stupidity.

"I'm so glad you got away today," Mabel said, her voice rich with emotion. "I've dreamed of coming here for so long." He knew, and for the last month, she'd been pressing him even harder about this trip.

This was his first chance to leave town. His work schedule had been hell as he transitioned to retiring at 68 from his accounting firm after more than thirty years. He also had a lot of community commitments. None of those situations should have kept him from doing this for the woman he loved so much. "I'm sorry for putting this off—"

"Nonsense!" She interrupted with a wave of her small hand. The skin was paper-thin, with blue veins visible. "Your life has been busy with the changes you're making. I understand that."

He saw her look out the window again, taking in the sight of the country road leading to Sunflower Farm. After her father died and her brothers all left the farm in a big hurry as soon as they could, she and her young husband had taken it over. They'd lived here in the middle of the Kansas prairie for sixty-three years. When his Uncle Howard had passed on, her heart hadn't been in staying there any longer. Lee hadn't wanted to take over the responsibilities of being a farmer. He'd already been in an accounting practice. But they hadn't wanted to sell the farm. They'd found another farmer to rent the land for running cattle on and raising wheat.

"I'm not sure what to expect regarding the farm." He hadn't been here for a while. The land renter kept up the field fences and the fields. He even used the barn for hay storage. The house had sat empty for nine years since Mabel had moved to town.

"Don't fret, dear. I know nobody has lived in or taken care of the old house." She looked out the side window.

He turned down the gravel country road leading to Sunflower Farm and memories washed over him. Some bad, like when storms had done serious damage at various times. They'd rebuilt the barn at least twice, an equipment shed, too. Most of the memories were good though. Most of those involving the gentle woman beside him.

The car became silent, both lost in a maelstrom of feelings tied to the old farm.

As Lee drove over the thick steel rods of the cattle guard and between the wire fence that could use repairs, he glanced at his aunt who stared forward now. Her lower lip trembled, and she put two bony fingers to it. He heard her suck in a shuddery breath.

"Are you all right?" He worried more about her with each passing second. "We don't have to go further." He stopped the Lexus sedan halfway up the dirt driveway.

She faced him, blinking her fading blue eyes. A lone tear slid down one wrinkled and pale cheek. "Oh, no, I don't want to leave." She swallowed hard and focused on the two-story, massive farmhouse. "It's so beautiful, isn't it?"

He saw a house that had been 'beautiful' years ago. Now the white paint was sparse, a lot of grayed boards revealed. Many of the long windows broken and boarded closed. The rounded tower on one side that his aunt had loved so much and filled with African Violets and other flowers suffered, too. The railings on the two porches where big white rocking chairs had always sat could use work, including painting. Her prized rosebushes that had lined the front sidewalk were now clumps of dead branches mixed with thriving weeds.

It disheartened him he'd let the house get so run down. Maybe he should have it razed. No. He couldn't do that but something needed done. He'd have to put thought into the matter now that he had some free time.

"Remember when you used to sleep out in the upstairs covered sun porch?" his aunt interrupted his musings. She giggled in that happy way she always had. "It used to drive your uncle nuts. You sleeping out there on a blanket instead of in a perfectly good bed."

Lee smiled, reaching over to gently squeeze her arthritic hand. "That was the fun about it. Making him crazy."

"You loved to test your limits." She smiled back, her eyes glimmering with amusement. "You would climb up on the roof to watch for falling stars at night. No matter how many times he warned you not to."

She shook her head at a memory, giggling. "Then one day you jumped from the hayloft onto a stack of hay bales... breaking your arm."

He laughed at the recollection. It hadn't been funny then. Her burning lecture had been worse than the broken bone. Her tears more so. He had scared her and he'd tried never to worry her like that again.

Lee's gaze shifted to the far side of the house to where a towering elm tree still held an old tire swing. His Uncle Howard had taken time from his endless chores to hang it for him. He'd also spent a lot of time he didn't have tossing a ball with him or teaching him how to drive their ancient farm truck. He'd talked to him about so many things. The man never tired of learning. He read any book he could get his hands on. He'd passed on the love of learning to Lee. His heart pinched at missing the big-hearted farmer.

"Remember when Uncle Howard..."

"Remember when your uncle..." she said at the same time.

They looked at each other and laughed together.

"There are a lot of memories here. Every one of them special. How about we go wander around? Share some of those memories."

Before they stepped from the car a dust-covered truck rattled over the cattle guard and headed toward them. Lee figured it was their land tenant coming to talk with them. Mabel had told him she'd called "P. Morgan" to tell the tenant that they would be at the farm today. He'd been okay with that. His communications with the tenant had been by mail or email since their original agreement. It was time to talk in person.

As the truck door opened, a slender woman in faded jeans and a blue chambray shirt eased out. She lifted her gaze to them and beamed. "Howdy, Lee! Mabel!"

He gaped in surprise at the still attractive woman he knew to be just a few years younger than himself, sixty-five. They'd met when her family bought the neighboring farm. The two families saw each other often after that although he'd spent more time with her than with her younger brother. He hadn't seen her in a long time. Not since the summer when they'd hung out a lot together before he'd gone off to the University of Kansas. She'd been too young for him to date but they'd been good friends. If she'd been older... If they'd both waited a few more years... But he'd met Linda his junior year and, well, she'd captured his heart.

"Patricia Kramer," he stated her name, feeling a sense of wonder. A strange moment of "What if" washed over him. There'd been times over the years when he'd wondered what had become of her. What if their friendship could have one day turned into more? Not that he regretted for a second his marriage with Linda.

She laughed, the big blue eyes he remembered as always sparkling with life shimmered with amusement. "It's Morgan now."

So, she'd gotten married. He shouldn't be surprised or disappointed. He grinned sheepishly. "I stand corrected."

Before he could ask why she was here now, she gave him a saucy, chastising look. "It's about time you made it back to the old farm."

Shame spread through him as he thought about the sorry shape of the house. "I had no idea that the house's condition had gotten this bad," he muttered, embarrassed. "The tenant renting the land never mentioned it. And I... Well, I should have checked on everything myself." A wave of guilt rolled over him.

She strode closer, her long silvery-white ponytail swinging behind her. She'd worn a ponytail way back then, too. He remembered flicking it in fun, or tugging on it, which usually made her frown at him and then laugh.

"I'm so glad you got your nephew out here," she said to Mabel as she climbed from the car.

Mabel walked toward her, opening her arms so that the two women hugged. "He's been busy."

"Life gets that way." Patricia nodded and grinned at Mabel. "Did you tell him what I want?"

Lee wasn't sure why, but his gut warned that something was up between these two. He raised an eyebrow when he noted a hint of mischief sparking in his aunt's expression. Yes, definitely something going on.

"Tell me what?" His aunt hadn't mentioned Patricia. "No offense, but why are you here?"

Patricia just smiled, seeming to wait for Mabel to explain.

His gaze shifted to his aunt, who looked to Patricia. Frustrated with whatever was going on between them, he pressed, "I thought you told me that our tenant would meet us here." He'd almost forgotten the part about the tenant wanting some kind of change in their agreement.

"Your tenant is here," Patricia said, drawing his attention. As he gaped at her in confusion, she added, "It's time I did more than just rent the land."

He blinked. "You are P. Morgan?" He had trouble wrapping his mind around the notion. "I thought the renter was Paul Morgan."

"Paul was my husband. He died five years ago." She jutted out her small chin. "Now 'P. Morgan' is Patricia Morgan. I took over our farm and using your land, too. With help from our oldest son, who took over my parents' farm."

Why hadn't he put one and one together and recognized her last name when she'd corrected him? It hadn't occurred to him. Seeing her again had unsettled him too much. "Guess you think I'm pretty dimwitted, not realizing you were—"

"Maybe," she teased with a smile. Then she went on, "Paul and I had a double-wide on our land." She motioned to the big Victorian behind him. "This is where I want to live."

"Why?"

Her cheeks grew pink, her eyes turned thoughtful. "Because I've never forgotten how warm and comforting this house used to be when I visited here." She glanced at his aunt. "Well, Mabel and Howard, too."

"That's sweet, dear." Mabel raised her gaze to Lee's; her aged-lined face filled with happiness. "Patricia wants to move into it, make it her home."

Patricia faced the house. "I want to give it some tender loving care. Get the place back to its former glory." She nodded toward what remained of the rose bushes. "Including Mabel's gardens."

Not that he opposed seeing the house he'd grown up in salvaged but the idea unsettled him, which was silly. Nobody had lived here in years. He didn't want to tear it down and he had a house in the city. This should be a good thing.

"I'm not ready to sell the farm." He looked toward his aunt and corrected himself. "Not that I have total say in that matter."

Mabel moved next to him, touched his arm. "She's not asking to take your old home away from you. She just wants to fix it up and move in. She wants to rent the house and the land."

"Seriously?" It was an interesting idea, a little strange, but interesting. "Why don't you want to buy it all?"

"I'm not ready for that step." She smiled. "Besides, you said you aren't ready to do that yet."

"True." His accountant mind went to finances. She already had a farm, a house there, and probably some kind of farm partnership with her son on her parents' old property. With all of that, she might not have the ability to get that kind of loan. Before he could catch himself, he said, "Maybe we could work out a loan where we carry—"

Her eyes sparked with amusement and she shook her head to cut him off. "Thanks, but no thanks." She didn't appear to have taken offense at his suggestion.

He gave a weak smile of apology. "Sorry. My business side popped out there for a second."

Mabel gently patted his arm. "It's okay, Lee, we understand. You couldn't help yourself. But Patricia and I know that isn't what you want right now."

It wasn't, still he felt... Well, he wasn't sure. For now, he'd accept Patricia making this old house into a home again. "I'll pay for the updating or whatever." Which was fair since he and Mabel weren't selling the property.

Patricia's smile grew, a hint of teasing flashed in her eyes. "How about offering old-fashioned elbow grease, too?"

That surprised him. "Help with the clean-up? Me?" He snorted. "I've never been the handyman sort. Oh, I can use tools...some of them, anyway." Put him in an office and he knew a lot and was comfortable there.

"I bet you can do more than you think," Patricia challenged. "I remember how you used to help your uncle with repairs around the farm."

He chuckled. "I'm not sure I was all that helpful. He was just a very patient man."

"That he was." Mabel gave Lee a loving glance. "Still, I think you can do more than you think, as Patricia said."

He supposed they were right. It might even be good for him, now that he had retired. "Better make sure my insurance is paid up."

With a roll of her eyes, Patricia shifted her focus to Mabel and both women grinned. "We'll need supervision with the project, from someone who knows every inch of the place."

Okay, he knew that. At least he had in the past.

"I can't come all the time," Mabel informed him with a playful look. "I have commitments to my dominoes group and to my scrapbooking pals. But you can bring me out here with you at least once a week."

"Lee, I really could use your help, at least on the simpler tasks," Patricia assured.

He studied her expression, she seemed serious now. His gut told him the two women had set him up, probably his aunt's doing. He knew Mabel worried about him since he wouldn't be going into an office every day. "What will you do with your time?" She'd asked him way more than once. Honestly, he didn't know. Work had been the focus of his life for years, even before his wife died. He didn't have hobbies, didn't play sports. He'd been a widow for ten years and hadn't been interested in having another relationship, hadn't thought he had the time to devote to it. Everything in his life was different now.

Patricia had mentioned 'simpler tasks.' That might be good for him. "Okay, I'm up for this. When do we start?"

The women seemed to sigh together in relief, then smiled in victory before hugging each other again. His wife had been a hugger, too. He mulled that over when Patricia moved to him, looked up in determination and drew him into a hug.

He froze and pulled in a surprised breath filled with the soft scent of roses and woman. Until that moment, he hadn't realized how much he missed a woman's touch. He wasn't sure what to do. Hug her back? Just endure it?

Mabel caught his attention, looking at him with gentleness. "It's okay, Lee. She means nothing by hugging you."

Patricia's arms were still around him and he didn't hate it. He remembered embracing her in friendship all those years ago. It had felt good and he'd been tempted to do more, like stealing a kiss. It wouldn't have been right. She'd been too young for him. But now...

She gave him a crooked grin, her eyes studying him. "Am I making you uncomfortable?"

"Maybe a little."

"We're not teenagers anymore. The age differences shouldn't matter." She continued watching him. "It's just a hug between friends. No pressure." Yet her gaze held interest, question.

What she said was true but he felt something shifting inside him. As if he was ready to step away from grieving the loss of his wife. Ten years was enough. Not that Patricia was pushing for more than just this momentary touch in friendship. Right?

He relaxed and allowed himself to give her a light hug before stepping back.

Mabel watched him, a hint of delight in her expression. He'd have to be careful she didn't get the wrong idea. Be careful neither of the women got the wrong idea.

Patricia turned toward the house, moving past the awkward moment. "I'm thinking a pale pink, with purple and turquoise trim."

Lee choked, blustered. "Hell no!"

Both women giggled at his horror. "Just teasing." Patricia grinned. "You need to lighten up, Lee."

He sighed. They would test him and enjoy every second. Oddly enough, he looked forward to it.

DARE TO DANCE

"I'm so glad you could come help us today," Dorothy said, filling coffee pots in the Senior Center's restaurant-style kitchen. "Help me, that is." She laughed. "The other women are too focused on trapping some man to dance with then."

"Trapping might be a bit harsh." Sarah Blythe chuckled too.

Dorothy turned to wink at her through black cat eye framed glasses and shrugged. "Just saying it like it is. As the young kids would say."

"Okay, you're right." She watched the other woman set a couple of glass pots on the stainless-steel counter. "Anyway, I'm happy to help."

She was but guilt weighed on her shoulders. "Even if I should be home finishing up the scarves I'm crocheting for my three granddaughters for Christmas."

As she watched her new friend, she thought about the big family get-together only two weeks away. There was still a lot of preparation work to help her oldest daughter. Everyone would go to her house this year. Yet when Dorothy had called, she jumped at the chance to come here this afternoon. The walls at home were closing in on her. Everywhere she turned there were memories of she and Alex.

"You'll get them done," Dorothy reassured her. She nodded to the hallway through the big kitchen window opening. "What do you think of the decorations?"

Red garland draped the hallway, sagging in one spot. Through the open doors across from the kitchen Sarah saw a scrawny tree decorated with a mixture of ornaments donated by the people who used the center. "You and the decorating committee did a good job."

The slightly battered angel on top was her own donation. It had been one of the numerous treetop angels she'd used on the family trees over the years.

The family trees. She leaned against the long counter and waited for the rush of pain to settle. She hadn't put up a Christmas tree in three years. Or had the family dinner at the old family house. She couldn't bear to do any of it without Alex helping or complaining she was doing too much. Oh, how the man had complained. She missed his grumping around. Missed knowing he went shopping on his own and stashed away gifts for everyone in the garage, all the while letting them think he was a Scrooge. They all knew better.

The pinch around her heart eased. So many good times together. Including those first few Christmases when they hadn't money to spare to buy even one gift for each other. Instead, they spent those Christmas mornings sitting together over a meager breakfast of eggs and toast. They shared their dreams of what future Christmas mornings would be like after they'd gotten better off after having the four kids both wanted.

Those memories, and the memories of the Christmas gatherings they had in their big old house, had haunted her days and nights. Memories were precious things unless they played with your heartstrings. Would she ever stop missing her husband? Alex had passed on three years ago, but it seemed like yesterday.

"Okay, the pots are ready for you," Dorothy advised and turned toward another task for the holiday party.

Sarah picked up one pot. Across the hall in the large recreation room, a handful of musicians were preparing their instruments. The guitar needed tuning, its off-key plunk almost hurting her ears. A second later the saxophone gave a rather strange squawk, followed by another horn she couldn't quite recognize. But when the pianist played a few chords, the piano sounded good. The group wasn't the best in the world but they were eager about playing today for the annual holiday dance. And from the sounds of conversations and laughter from the growing number of people, everyone was excited about the party.

In college, she and Alex had gone dancing every chance they could. Over the years, other things got in their way. She'd missed it but often danced around the house as she did her household chores… still did now and then. He always said she had "dancing feet." Sarah wasn't sure she could dance today without thinking about him. Maybe no one would even ask her to dance. She'd be satisfied just watching the refreshment table and keeping the coffeepots filled.

******

Tom Williamson's nose felt frozen and his toes burnt to a crisp, yet he didn't complain. It would only hurt his old army buddy's feelings. He would never do that. Pete loved this ancient Ford Mustang with all its eccentricities—including the defroster that had given up defrosting years ago and the heater that only blew out hot air on the floorboard. At least it was transportation. And he would not spend another dreary winter afternoon at home watching all that mind-numbing nonsense on television.

"You'll like the gang." Pete glanced across at Tom as he turned into the parking lot of the Senior Center. "Couple of 'em don't hear so well anymore and one can't see hardly at all. Still, they can all wield a mean cue stick."

Tom hadn't played pool since before joining the service near the start of the Vietnam War, a good fifty-some years ago. He'd balked about coming here. Such a place was for "old" people. At seventy-one, he wasn't "old" but he didn't get around as good as he used to do. Pete persisted in whittling away at him. His friend called him a fool for not getting out of the house more. Since losing his darling Abigail two years ago, he had not felt like socializing.

Pete grumbled under his breath about so many cars in the parking lot today. He steered into the last available space, right next to a yard-high pile of snow. "I'll tell them to take it easy on you." He chuckled, a gravely sound after years of smoking. "I won't. Been looking forward to beating the daylights out of ya."

"Don't get your hopes up, old man." Tom flashed his friend a teasing look. He shifted to muscle open the door that had a tendency to stick. "I might be rusty but I can still take the likes of you."

Tom eased around the snow pile and met up with Pete at the back bumper. At the same time a pair of white-haired ladies drove down their lane, searching the lot for a space. He thought of Abigail. Her hair had turned pure white in her fifties. She complained about it, talked about coloring it back to blond again but never had. He hadn't cared at all and would have loved her if she'd gone bald. He sure missed her.

"Should have known what this crowd was here for," Pete muttered. "You stick close, pal, and I'll get you to safety right quick."

Before Tom could even question him, he watched Pete ignore the arthritis that plagued his knees and all but sprint toward the back door of the center. Tom took off after him, wondering what irritated his friend.

"What were you talking about? Safety?" he asked as Pete struggled with opening the heavy metal door.

As if Tom had no sense at all, Pete nodded toward the doorway leading into the recreation room. Slightly off-key music filled the air and the sounds of women's voices—a lot of women's voices.

"It's one of their dance days, I guess. Dangerous time for a widowed man." He shifted into high gear again and strode into the building, heading down the hallway and avoiding even looking toward the big room.

Tom stepped inside, glad to have warmth surrounding him again. He ambled down the hallway with its holiday decorations, feeling wistful. He and Abigail used to go out a lot when they were younger. They always loved dancing, letting their wild sides out. His wife shimmied and shook all over the dance floor. And he sure liked holding her close for a slow dance. But those days were over. He'd lost his dance partner, his life partner. He didn't want another one. A man could only love so deep one time in his life. If he got that chance. He'd loved Abigail for forty-nine years… still loved her.

"You coming or not?" Pete questioned in irritation from the other end of the hallway.

Tom jerked back to the moment, surprised he'd stopped outside the party room and stood tapping his foot to the music. "Be right there." He moved forward once more, his attention still sidetracked by the enticing sounds of laughter and music.

The door from the kitchen flew open and would have knocked him flat if Tom hadn't jumped away just in time. In the next instant, a gray-haired, slender woman only shoulder height to him bustled into his path. The smell of something flowery assailed him. He froze.

"Oh gosh! I'm sorry. Guess I was in too big of a hurry," she apologized and gave him a dimpled smile. She held up a coffeepot in one hand. "They've been complaining about needing more coffee."

He should say something but her anxious babble and warm blue eyes had him standing there like an idiot.

******

Sarah studied the man with a head of thick, dark hair dappled with gray. His face was lean but he still took a woman's breath away. She didn't remember seeing him around the center before. He gaped at her after her rushed apology, stayed silent, and she grew concerned.

"Did I hit you with the door? Are you hurt?" She swept her gaze up and down his much taller form. As far as she could tell he didn't appear damaged. In fact, even wearing a heavy winter coat, he looked to be in good physical shape for a man in his late 60s or early 70s. If he were coming to the dance, the women would swarm all over him. Poor man.

When she looked up again and their eyes met, he shook his head. "I'm fine. You startled me is all."

She liked the sound of his deep voice and the crooked smile he'd given her. Her stomach felt funny, like when she first met Alex. Which was silly. She was too old for having romantic thoughts of any kind, especially about a man she didn't even know. Still, she returned his smile, and it felt good.

"There are two coffeepots to take to the rec room. Could you help me?" Why had she asked him that? When she spotted Pete Townsend at the end of the hallway waiting for this man, she was sure the man wasn't even going to the party. Pete avoided the dances and any gatherings with the women here.

The stranger took the pot she'd been holding. "It would please me to help you."

Now he was studying her and she hoped her red dress looked okay, that she hadn't spilled something on it already, that it wasn't too tight. Was her hair all right? She'd been bustling around a lot since she arrived. She hoped her hair wasn't standing on end in some weird way. Then she realized her crazy thoughts and her cheeks warmed.

You're acting like a teenager. Stop it!

"Thanks." She headed back into the kitchen for the second coffeepot. "I'm Sarah," she called over her shoulder. "Sarah Blythe."

******

Tom watched in amusement as the pretty woman blushed and then hurried away from him. He looked down the hallway and found Pete glowering at him.

"What are ya doing?" Pete asked, heading his way but stopping a safe distance from the open recreation room door and the kitchen. "Put that thing down. Or Sarah will drag you into that room." As he glanced at the room that worried him, his frown deepened. "Ya won't get away from those women. No sirree. They'll be all over ya, like flies to flypaper."

The kitchen door swung open once more, and Sarah stepped out. Her gently lined cheeks were still a little pink, which Tom found charming. But she smiled up at him, then towards Pete, who glowered in return.

She shook her head at Pete in chastisement and lifted her gaze to Tom. "Despite your friend's accusation, the women inside won't harm you. But if you need me to, I'll protect you." With a last glance at Pete, she headed for the party room and assumed Tom would follow her.

Pete hazarded a step forward. "Don't go in there! I'm warning you again. Don't. Go." His gaze slid toward the room, his expression showing he feared a woman would spot him and drag him inside.

For the first time in over two years, Tom laughed. Really laughed. Whether it was from Pete's distress about the women or this tiny female protecting him from anything at all, he didn't know. But it felt good to laugh. Then, as though his Abigail was standing next him, he sensed her approval. It was time to enjoy life again. He could spin another woman around the dance floor. Nothing had to come of it beyond having fun together.

"I'll play with the guys another time."

"But—"

Tom shook his head and cut off his friend. "Another time."

With a wave to send Pete on his way, Tom took another couple of seconds to think. Had he made the right decision? Maybe he should... Buck up, buddy. You've been in battle. You've seen the worst in humans. This is just some sweet ladies wanting to have a good time.

At last he moved in Sarah's direction. As he walked into the large room, everyone looked at him. He felt uneasy, considered going to find Pete. You're tougher than that. It wasn't only women and the small band in here. There were maybe a dozen men. A few appeared relieved at having another man join their midst, being outnumbered by women what looked like three or four to one. Two men didn't seem as friendly toward him. Apparently, they liked to be the center of attention. He was competition. Not that he felt that way.

He stood in place for too long because a group of eight women was bee lining in his direction. His heart raced in panic. Sweat beaded between his shoulder blades and on his upper lip. Don't show fear.

He'd learned that in combat all those years ago. Not fear. It's the coat, is all. Still, his pulse ratcheted up another notch.

Where was Sarah? He glanced around, trying not to feel desperate. When he spotted her standing by a long table next to the wall setting her coffee pot down, relief calmed him. She turned and seemed to look for him. That made him feel even better. He gave a weak smile.

She gazed past him and must have seen the pack of all-too-eager-looking ladies behind him. A twinkle her eyes, she walked toward him. "Thought I lost you for a minute," she said. "Or you chased after Pete to go upstairs to the safety of the pool room."

He shook his head and headed in her path. "Just slow is all."

He followed her back to the table where coffee pots, a punch bowl, and dozens of plates of cookies sat lined up. The sound of the other women's retreating steps and grumbles was music to his ears. "Glad you spotted me." Oh, so glad.

As she faced him, her expressive eyes showed her understanding. She smiled and took the coffee pot from him and set it on the hot plate beside the pot she'd carried in. "Told you I would protect you."

He chuckled, then remembered he hadn't even introduced himself. "I'm Tom. Tom Williamson."

She held out a slender hand. "Pleased to meet you, Tom."

He couldn't remember the last time he'd shaken a woman's hand. He took her hand in his, felt the softness of hers against his slightly calloused palm. A nice feeling, much like when he held Abigail's hand. He thought he should feel odd or guilty holding another woman's hand, but he didn't.

Behind them, the band started up a slow song meant for dancing. He released Sarah's hand as he watched her worry her wistful glance turned toward the dance floor where many couples had gathered.

Heat crawled up his face, but he asked in a rush, "Will you dance with me?"

"I…" She seemed torn with indecision. "I didn't come here to dance today. I came because my friend nagged me into coming with her."

Something they had in common. Tom tugged off his coat while she watched him. "Pete has been annoying me for months to come here with him. I finally caved in. Needed to get out of the house."

The look of understanding she gave him lightened his heart. She didn't appear set on chasing after him, like some other ladies had looked. She was just a nice lady. Small talk had never been his best thing but he gave it a shot.

"My Abigail and I used to love dancing." He swallowed hard and hung his coat on one hook nearby on the back wall.

Sarah moved next to him, whispering, "My Alex and I did too." She giggled and blushed. "Fact is, I often dance around my house while doing my housework. Silly, I know."

He felt her sadness at having lost someone she loved. Yet he also felt her strength. She was moving on with her life, including coming here today to socialize when she didn't feel like it. She was a good example to follow. Better than Pete, who couldn't find the courage even to consider sharing time with another woman since his wife had died several years ago. Tom wouldn't shy away from life like Pete, not any longer.

"I promise not to step on your feet." He smiled down at Sarah. "At least not too many times."

She hesitated, gave him a sassy grin. "Guess I'll take my chances." Then she took his hand and led him toward the dance floor.

The emptiness he'd experienced for so long didn't feel so bad now. Gut instinct told him he'd found more than a dancing partner for the afternoon but he wouldn't rush into anything. He sensed she wouldn't want to, either. For now, having this lovely woman beside him as he re-entered life was enough.

FINDING THEIR WAY AGAIN

"I'm home!" Karen called out as she walked into the laundry room from the garage. "Did you hear me?"

Another busy day going from one community meeting to another had tired her. It would have been nice to get a cheery, "Glad you're back!" or even a distracted, "What did you say?" Instead, she got no response.

With a sigh, she put her purse on the dryer as was her habit. As she stepped into the kitchen, spotting the dish washing soap container on the counter. Instinct told her Mike had set it there, maybe added a pod but did not turn on the dishwasher. Somehow the third part of the process rarely connected with him.

A quick glance inside told her she'd been right. She loved the man but sometimes... She turned the machine on and then listened to make sure all was okay. Like the other appliances, the dishwasher was nearing twenty-years old. One of these days, they would have to replace them, the refrigerator first. It only made ice when it was in the mood. And the freezer had a tendency to add a layer of frost over things at least once a month.

She pushed those potential problems to the back of her mind. Too much to deal with right now. Her feet hurt, and she felt brain dead after the lively discussions at meetings today. All she'd wanted on getting home was peace. A warm welcome would have been nice too.

A bit down, she went into the living room. The over-stuffed chair with the big footstool by the window called to her. Her current embroidery project waited for her on the end table. It was one of several craft projects she'd started and needed to finish up. Lately she'd been better at starting a new one than in focusing enough to finish anything. She felt like she was in some kind of limbo.

Across the room, her husband had a baseball game on the large screen TV. The sound turned up too high for her comfort. Mike dozed stretched out in his recliner, oblivious to the game and her. He worked hard at his job as an insurance adjuster, harder after the summer storms with occasional hailstorms, like the most recent one. She understood how exhausted he got. At least he'd got two days off from the latest craziness. He needed the rest.

She kept busy too. Still, she looked forward to their evenings together, as few as they seemed to be these days. Between his long work hours and her community commitments... Well, time together was a rarity.

He gave a shuddery snort but didn't awaken. Disappointment curled through Karen. She could have said something, could have touched his arm and gotten his attention. Yet she did nothing except pick up her embroidery hoop and ease into her comfortable chair. She wouldn't even bother to change the channel. Noise in the background was enough for her.

She blew out a sigh and pulled out the embroidery needle. How many times had she done this? Settled down to work on some project with her heart not into it. Wanting to talk about this or that with Mike, with him having fallen asleep. Without having the energy to disturb him. It felt like this had been going on for at least a year. Maybe longer.

She loved him and knew he loved her. They fit together after forty-two years of marriage. Each of them had their own interests, their own jobs... their own lives.

Their own lives. The notion had surprised her but, now considering it, the statement was true. That made her heart sick. How had they grown so far apart? Why had they allowed this to happen? This wasn't the image that either of them had envisioned when they'd fallen in love and got married.

Mike's cell phone came to life next to him on the end table covered with his collection of remotes and magazines. He jerked awake and grabbed it, glancing at the caller ID. "Yeah, I'm glad you called. I tried to get hold of you earlier today." He hesitated, listening. "Sure. I'll meet you there in a half hour."

Karen's stomach tightened and she concentrated on not poking her finger with the sharp needle. He would meet his friends again. She didn't begrudge him that but what about her? Sure, he liked to talk politics and about the latest sports news with his friends. Topics that weren't her best subjects of conversation. Now, if he wanted to talk about what was happening with one of her community groups, what she'd been doing in their gardens, or about one of her craft projects, or… She realized they didn't know how to talk to each other anymore.

He flicked the TV off without even asking her if she wanted to watch something. Then he stood, stretched from side to side, and glanced around the room. His eyes widened at seeing her in her chair. His reaction made her sadder. "You don't care if I go meet the gang, right?" he asked, sounding torn between uncertainty and eagerness.

She wanted to snap, "Yes, I care!" Instead, she bit down her protest and gave him a forced smile before looking down. "No. I plan to work on this gift." The same one she'd been working on well past the time to give the gift for her daughter's last birthday.

"You're always welcome to join us." He went to the closet for his favorite ball cap, seldom going anywhere without it. He'd told her that many times and she knew his friends would be okay with her joining them. The key here being they were his friends. She didn't want to intrude on their time together.

"Thanks, but I'm fine here." Just me and this stupid project.

As usual, he didn't mention her going with him again. Tears stung her eyes. All she had to do was open her mouth and ask him to stay. Instead she sat there in uncomfortable silence while he prepared to leave her alone for yet another night. Usually, it didn't bother her. Or had she become so used to this happening?

He walked over to her, gave her a quick peck on the mouth—not even enough to call it a kiss. As he flashed her a smile of goodbye and headed from the room, his thoughts were already on meeting his friends. She sat numb and lonely.

Your own fault. You could have stopped Mike from going. But pride kept her from asking him to stay with her. What were they going to do about this growing distance between them? She wasn't miserable enough in the marriage to want out. Was he? Or had Mike even noticed what had happened to them?

A lone tear slipped down her cheek. Working on the project tonight no longer interested her. She might as well get ready for bed, crawl between the covers and read for a while. She didn't even feel like watching one of her recorded shows or checking for something new on Netflix. Boy, she was in full pity-herself mode and she hated it. She wasn't that unhappy with her life. But sometimes... Well, sometimes she got a little down.

******

The dishwasher was going as Mike strode through the kitchen, like it had just started. Karen. No doubt she'd discovered when she'd come home, he'd failed to turn it on earlier. He'd meant to but got distracted when he'd heard the crowd at the ballgame he'd been watching on TV get excited over someone who hit a home run.

He noticed her purse on the dryer, knowing she'd get it later. She often set it down there when she got home. When had she gotten home? He must have been zonked out. He'd been so tired. Too many insurance cases to deal with since that last big storm. Good for his business but tough on a man in his sixties.

His thoughts turning to seeing his friends, he hurried into the garage and his Ford Ranger. One of these days he needed to get it washed. He glanced at his wife's SUV. Okay, he needed to get hers cleaned too.

He climbed into his Ranger, backed out of the garage and hesitated before closing the door. Something in Karen's eyes hadn't seemed right, at least in that second she'd looked at him. As usual, she'd not voiced a problem with him going to see his friends. If she'd asked him to stay home, he would have. But she never asked. Still, there had been something different in her expression, her attitude tonight. He wasn't the quickest to pick up on women's emotions and he knew that. Maybe he was over-thinking this.

Listening to the garage door squeak its way closed, he eased onto the street. Should he change his plans? Should he stay here with his wife? No, she'd said she would work on some gift she was making. She didn't need him. Sometimes he felt like she never needed him.

******

The next week passed in a blur of activity. Karen and Mike were like those two ships that passed each other in the night. She went from one community meeting to another, squeezing in time to be with her sister. Her sister asked why she seemed down. Karen had told her there was just too much going on and it tired her. She didn't think her sister had bought that excuse this time and yet she hadn't pressed her, which she'd been thankful about. What troubled her was only between her and Mike.

Her cell phone rang as she pulled into the grocery store parking lot to pick up a few things to cook tonight. This morning Mike had told her that he planned to be home earlier than usual. She would make his favorite meal: lasagna, garlic bread, and a big salad.

The phone rang again as she eased into a space. Mike's ring tone. Disappointment slid through her but she tried to ignore it and act upbeat. "Do you want anything from the grocery store?"

"Uh... Not that I can think of." He spoke to someone else with him in his office and then returned to her. "Todd and the others will get sushi tonight. I'll go, too. Give you some free time to work on that gift you've wanted to get finished. Is that all right?"

"Well, I had planned..." She closed her eyes and swore she wouldn't act the needy wife. "Sure, go ahead. I'll just pick up fast-food for myself tonight and... and work on that project while I watch TV." She'd told him when they'd spoken this morning that she wanted to make something special tonight. He'd forgotten, maybe not even heard what she'd said.

He took a second. "Are you sure? I don't have to go. We can—"

"Go!" she cut him off, annoyed. "I'll be fine." Had he caught the frustration in her voice? She doubted it but she didn't want him to feel guilty. "It's not a problem." She didn't want him staying home to be with her out of pity.

Again, he hesitated before saying, "All right, if you're sure. I'll see you around eight or nine."

He hung up, and she wanted to toss the phone on the car's floor. That would have been a childish reaction. She needed to buck up and forget this latest set back in her hope to spend more time with her husband. You would think she had been PMSing for the last month with her focusing so much on her loneliness. But that part of her female life had ended, thank goodness. The mood swings continued though. Maybe she needed to talk to her doctor about them.

******

Mike frowned into space after ending the call. Okay, he might be dense sometimes but Karen's shout of "Go!" raised a serious red flag. The additional "I'll be fine" was the waving of that flag.

He thought about their many years of marriage. They never fought. They had their disagreements. But when Karen didn't want to continue on with an argument, she clammed up or walked away. When he tried to press her to see if he'd said something wrong or find out if he'd hurt her somehow, she had this annoying way of clipping, "I'm fine!" or "It's fine!" Which he'd learned meant the opposite.

Resigned, he called Todd. He didn't care about the sushi, anyway. But he cared about Karen and knew he belonged at home tonight.

******

Karen put the last of the groceries away and looked at the sack of tacos she'd picked up. They held no appeal. She wasn't interested in eating another meal alone. She'd skip the cold tacos for now. Taking a nice long bubble bath and finishing the mystery book she'd started the other day sounded good. Anything but sitting in front of the television alone again or sitting in her favorite chair and trying to add a few more stitches to the embroidery project she'd started to hate.

She went to the bedroom and stood next to the dresser. The mirror caught her attention. Who was that woman looking back at her? When had those thin wrinkles developed on her chin, around her mouth, at the corners of her eyes? She looked more like her mother every day. Not when her mother had been a young, vital woman, either. When her mother had grown older. The thought was alarming.

As she studied the changes, she wondered if they were why Mike spent less and less time with her. The face in the mirror was not the young woman he'd married. Nor was the rest of her body anything like what it had been when she'd been twenty-one on their wedding day. But Mike had changed too. His hair had gotten thinner; his body pudgier; his shoulders slumping. Not that she cared about any of that. He was still the man she loved… would always love.

She removed the thin silver-chained necklace with the tiny peanut charm that her daughter had given her last Christmas. Then she took off her wedding ring as she always did when taking a bath. She told herself to snap out of this depression. She had a good life, wonderful grown children, friends she cherished, and a husband she would never trade.

The sound of the garage door squeaking as it raised snagged her attention. She froze, thinking she needed to remind Mike that it needed oiling. Mike! What was he doing here already? Had they canceled the dinner thing tonight? Usually, he called when that happened and often to say he thought he'd go back to the office and work a little longer.

Happiness skittered through her, wariness too. She didn't move, waited, wondered.

She heard Mike's footsteps clapping against the wood floor in the dining room, padding over the living room carpet. Still she waited, wondered.

"Karen? You in the bedroom?" He sounded anxious.

"Yes." She heard her breathless voice. Her heart raced. Don't get your hopes up. He'll tell you he and his friends are getting together later than they'd planned.

Mike stepped into the doorway, his still handsome face—at least to her—looking tight with concern. His gaze swept over her with all the intensity it once had. Her body reacted to him as it once had, too. Yet she didn't move, didn't want to take a chance on saying something wrong.

His expression calmed, and he blew out an uneven breath. He stood there not speaking, just studying her.

"What are you doing here?"

"I had to come home." He held her gaze. "Something I can't explain told me this was where I needed to be tonight. With you."

Hope swelled within her. "You don't have to do this. I know how much you like sushi and eating out with your friends from work."

He walked toward her, determined. Her heart shuddered. At the tender look in his eyes, her knees grew weak as they had in the past.

Stopping toe-to-toe with her, he cupped her face with both hands, making sure she looked at him. "You mean much more to me than sushi or getting together with anyone else."

He smoothed a thumb over her cheek, rubbing at a tear that had slipped out. "I'm not the quickest at picking up things sometimes, emotions and feelings." He laughed at himself without real amusement. "But you've known that for years."

She did; she swallowed a painful lump. "It's okay, I…"

Regret spread over his lightly lined face. "I'm sorry. I work hard at making my business a success. I even work hard at keeping up with my friends."

His thumb slid over her lips. "But what matters most in my life—

you—I keep letting down." He thumbed her lips again. "And I'm sorry."

Karen watched him, shocked. He rarely did anything touchy-feely. "I'm sorry, too. Let's do something about it, okay?"

She pulled in a breath, savored his continued touch. "I'll work less on my projects. I'll…" His tender smile made her stop talking.

He studied her. "My work schedule is slowing down. Think you could rearrange your commitments to take a week off with me? We can go anywhere you want."

"A vacation?" She couldn't remember when they'd gone away for more than a long weekend. Mike was a homebody. If she traveled, it was with one of her friends, sometimes with their daughter.

"An honest-to-goodness vacation," he reiterated. "Maybe even a cruise, like you go on with your travel pals."

She knew how much he detested cruises, so this was a huge step for him. Tears clogged her throat. When she could speak again, she said with a crooked smile, "Maybe just a driving trip somewhere. Anywhere. I don't care."

His relief at not being forced to go on a cruise shown in his eyes. "We'll figure it out together."

They would be all right. They would find their way again.

THE WISHING TREE

"Dad, why don't you come here for dinner tonight?"

Before Sam Johnson could respond to his son's offer, his daughter-in-law called out, "We've got a meeting at church tonight."

"Sorry, Dad," Eric sounded annoyed and resigned. "Maybe this weekend instead."

"Sure. We'll see about sometime this weekend." Sam didn't hold much hope for that either. His son and family were constantly on the go to something or other. "Besides, I've been thinking about…" What? "About calling my buddy to go bowling tonight." Not really, but he didn't want his son to feel bad.

"That's great! You two haven't done that in a long time." Eric hesitated, seeming to listen to something his wife said in the background. "Gotta go. Sorry."

Sam was starting to hate the word sorry. He heard it far too often from his grown kids. "Sorry I haven't called you." "Life's been crazy, sorry." "We have to cancel on Sunday dinner again, sorry."

He ended the call and shoved the cell phone in his jean's pocket. His gaze slid to the morning newspaper spread out on the kitchen table. He'd already checked the obituaries and, no, he hadn't been listed. Nor had he recognized any of the names there. Pitiful, reading the obits. His wife had done that, watching for people she'd known in the community or from their church. She'd always been one of the first to offer condolences to family left behind or to offer help in any way she could. He'd kept up the ritual, although he rarely did more than maybe attend a funeral. He needed to stop that depressing habit.

One habit he'd gotten into that he would continue was going to Stanford Park for a morning walk, at least when his body cooperated. It had become somewhere he escaped to when the confines of his house became too much for him. Six rooms filled with nothing but things. Other than his own, no voices echoed around those rooms. There was no laughter, no shared conversations, no minor disagreements followed by "I'm sorry" or "You were right." There was nothing but silence and remembered conversations in his head.

As always, an ache squeezed his chest. Ever since he had lost the other half of him, dear Evelyn, he didn't know what to do in the house that was no longer a home. So, he went to the nearby park.

He grabbed his light jacket from the hall tree beside the front door. After locking the door, he did a quick, short knee bend. Good. The arthritis in his knees seemed okay this morning. He never knew and had learned to check before he walked to the park.

******

Rosie sat at the table in the senior center's reception area sipping a cup of coffee. Two other women around her age sat with her, chatting with each other about their grandchildren. They were old friends and nice enough but she still felt like an outsider here. She'd only started coming to the center a few weeks ago after moving into a nearby apartment complex. Making new friends took time and she understood that.

A man in his eighties sat on a sofa behind her, snoring. It made her smile and remember how her husband could snore loud enough to wake the dead. At least that's how she'd teased him. Her heart hurt at the memory. Memories could be hurtful and wonderful too.

She chugged the last of her coffee. Time to get moving. She'd stopped in here to see what was going on activity-wise that day before she went to walk around the park in which the center sat. "Want to join me on my walk?" she asked the ladies, already knowing their answer, but always believing it polite to ask.

Both shook their heads. "My hip is acting up today," one said. "My feet are kind of swollen today," the other said.

Rosie stood and returned her cup to the small kitchen area. With a smile she headed for the front door. "Maybe next time." She doubted it but you never knew for sure.

She went out to her car where her precious poodle, Frenchie, waited for her return. They were walking companions. Sometimes Frenchie wanted to run but she gave in to Rosie's refusal to do so. Running wasn't something she did anymore. Well, she'd never been a runner, not even a jogger.

******

On his second lap around the park Sam spotted the older woman standing next to a water fountain. She wore a familiar bright pink sweatsuit and a patient expression. Her white, curly-haired poodle was busy sniffing around the fountain's base.

"Good morning," he called out. "Nice day isn't it?"

When she didn't acknowledge him by even looking in his direction, he kept on walking. He didn't think she'd heard him. Maybe her hearing was as bad as his sometimes. Getting older wasn't easy. Anyway, it pleased him to see her back in his park.

He had first seen her here a month ago and he'd watched for her every day since. There had only been a couple of times when he hadn't seen her. It had been around the first day of spring. He'd sensed a kindred spirit in this unknown woman with a face gently creased by time. He snorted. When did I become so poetic? Evelyn would have laughed herself silly at the idea.

Sam continued walking, continued thinking about the stranger. The air of sorrow that hung about her sometimes and the droop to her shoulders got to him. Sometimes she looked wistful; at other times lost. He knew those feelings well. Did anyone else see those reactions to life in him?

His feet kept moving him down the cracked sidewalk. The exercise so familiar that his body didn't need his full concentration. Unless he almost stumbled.

Did she, too, force herself out of bed each morning and sit down at a table meant for two or for a family now grown and gone? Did she read the newspaper from cover to cover to fill the time like he did? He wished he could do more than exist from day to day. It would be nice to have someone with whom he could share his memories, someone to understand what he was going through. He had great kids who cared about him but they couldn't grasp how he felt. As he'd often heard said, "They weren't walking in his shoes."

Miss Pinkie, as he'd grown to think of her, caught his attention again. She settled onto the bench beneath the towering fruit-less mulberry tree he loved to watch change with the seasons. The tree's widespread branches and thick, green canopy of leaves offered shade to people who strolled through the park. Sometimes it provided a place for nests of chirping baby robins, a haven for twittering sparrows, or a place for squawking crows to protest the invasion of their territory. It held proof that life continued. He liked that most about this tree.

She must like it, too, for she often sat there to catch her breath during her morning walk.

The early April morning's cool breeze whispered through the oaks, elms and cottonwoods. The soft wind caressed Sam's already heated body. He saw it blow chin-length hair into Miss Pinkie's face. She reached up a hand to shove the strands away before she looked in his direction.

"Beautiful day," she said to him, smiling when she noticed him.

Even though his eyesight wasn't the best it had ever been, he saw the soft curve to her mouth. She'd given him other gentle smiles when they'd seen each other in the park. He looked forward to experiencing it. Each time, the warmth in it made him feel good. It shoved the coldness of his days away and made him wish for the chance to encounter happiness like he'd felt when Evelyn was alive.

"Perfect," he answered. He returned her smile, knowing her eyes would twinkle and her cheeks turn a pretty shade of pink. He'd seen the reaction close a few times and found it appealing.

She bent down to pat the poodle at her feet. The dog looked up at her in adoration. Maybe he should get a dog, so he'd have company around the house. He'd never had one. He wouldn't get a poodle though. A German shepherd? A Labrador?

His gaze moved to the tree. Peace washed over him as always. He felt even more tranquil when she sat beneath its protective branches. One day, maybe he'd find the courage to sit beside her and ask her what she thought about the tree. Maybe he'd even ask if he could join her on her walk around the park.

******

Rosie saw the familiar older man striding down the sidewalk nearby. They'd seen each other many times, but somehow had never spoken more than a casual, "Good morning" or "Nice day." She suspected he was shy, kept to himself. Even now she'd called out about the beautiful day and he'd responded with one word: "Perfect." But he'd added a smile this time. Progress, she supposed.

She liked the looks of him, except he seemed to carry a sadness, something she was too acquainted with herself. If she didn't have Frenchie to keep her busy feeding, petting, and walking, some days she might not even get out of bed. That was a ridiculous thought. She never let anything keep her down for long. But losing Hank two years ago right after Christmas had been a blow. His death had been unexpected. She hadn't even had time to say a final goodbye because someone had stolen him from her in that awful car accident.

A warm breeze drifted over her where she sat on a park bench beneath a favorite tree. Frenchie gave a little yip and tugged at her chain. The poodle could get impatient.

"Okay, okay." She glanced down at her cherished pet and then over at the man still watching her. His continued gaze as he stood there in silence didn't make her the least bit uncomfortable.

She gave him another smile and, as he'd done moments ago, he returned it. This time she thought maybe his smile reached his eyes. More progress. The realization brightened her mood. She looked forward to seeing him here at the park. Someday she would like to talk to him. When he was ready. When she was ready.

******

Sam grimaced, growing more distraught with each step he took along the park's sidewalk. Miss Pinkie wasn't here today. He hadn't seen her in more than a week and he'd worried about her. Was she sick? Did she have anyone to care for her? People needed someone when they were feeling poorly. They needed someone when the solitude became too much to bear. Why hadn't he given her his telephone number in case she needed help?

He grumbled to himself about being an old fool. Dagnabit, he'd had the perfect opportunity that day when they'd talked about the "beautiful day." Why hadn't he gotten past his uneasiness with stepping out of his tendency to keep a distance from others? They'd shared friendly smiles. And he'd noted the encouraging look in her eyes. Had he "manned up," like his grandson would say? Nope.

Because that would have been moving way too fast. And socially he moved at a turtle's pace. Not that he wanted anything more than friendship with someone he suspected had a lot in common with him.

He glanced at his wishing tree, which didn't seem as sparkling with life today. Maybe it missed her, too.

******

"I'm going back to the senior center today. Going to walk around the park," Rose told her daughter over the phone. She'd hated not going to the park this last week but a late spring cold had taken the energy from her.

"Have you talked to your doctor about getting out again?" Theresa sounded worried. "You shouldn't rush things."

Her kids and her doctor had told her to keep close to home until she got over the cold. They had feared it progressing to pneumonia. So, she'd stayed in the house that felt so empty, taking care of the stupid cold, and letting Frenchie out in the fenced backyard. Both had missed their park.

"I'm fine," Rosie stated with determination. "I need to get out of this house. You don't have to worry about me."

She heard her daughter sigh, accepting that she would not change Rosie's mind. "Be sure to call me if—"

"I will call if I need you," Rosie cut Theresa off, smiling to herself. Sometimes her daughter acted more like a mother to her than a daughter.

As she hung up, she glanced around the living room of her new apartment. Moving from Lincoln, Nebraska where she and Hank had lived most of their forty-five years of marriage had been tough. Selling the family home even harder. But it was good to be closer to her daughter and grandkids. At least she still had the main pieces of furniture that meant anything to her.

While she'd been sick with the annoying cold, she'd curled up in Hank's recliner, watching old Westerns like he'd enjoyed and then baseball games. She'd never been fond of either the Westerns or sports. Now they'd felt comforting. But she'd wondered what "her friend from the park"—as she thought of him—watched on TV, if he watched television. He sometimes wore a Royals ball cap, so maybe he watched baseball. Why hadn't she ever taken that step to speak with him? They could have sat on the bench they both seemed to favor and talked about… well, anything.

She caressed Frenchie in her lap. "We're going to the park tomorrow."

When Frenchie gave an excited yip, Rosie chuckled. "I'm thinking we might even introduce ourselves to our shy friend."

******

A long, desolate day later, Sam returned to Stanford Park. Winded after the six-block walk from his house, he stopped at the timeworn drinking fountain a dozen feet from his mulberry tree. The birds sang extra loud today. The sun glowed a little brighter than usual. Contemplating the reason the air appeared so much more alive, he sensed someone behind him.

Straightening his slightly arthritic back, Sam wiped water drops from the corner of his mouth with the back of his hand. He turned and towered over Miss Pinkie, who stood a good six inches shorter. His stomach quivered just as it had the first time he'd met Evelyn.

"It's a marvelous morning." She beamed up at him. Her poodle strained at the leash, paying more attention to the water fountain.

Sam stared at her blue eyes, accented by tiny crow's feet at the corners. He was sure that years of smiling and laughter had formed those lines. Those eyes scrutinized him, waiting for his response. What the devil had she said? He felt like an idiot.

"It's already warm for so early in the day." The words sounded boring. He gave a nervous smile. "Sorry. I'm out of practice with proper socialization." At least with anyone other than his family or his best friend, who he didn't see much of these days.

Her expression softened with understanding, but she didn't comment on his remark. She lifted one age-spotted hand to dab at the gleam of sweat on her brow. "The day is warm. I suppose it's time to stop wearing this old sweatsuit but I love it." She glanced down for a second. "My dear, departed husband gave it to me a few years ago for my birthday."

He heard the sorrow in her tone, saw the shimmer of tears that she fought back. As she hadn't remarked on his "out of practice" apology, he didn't speak to her obvious grief. Instead he took in that they had something in common besides being well past the age of twenty, even sixty. They had both lost their life mates.

Sam nodded down at his scuffed-looking gray walking shoes. "I understand. My sweet Evelyn bought me these shoes a while back for Father's Day. My granddaughter says they look like bowling shoes, not walking shoes." He shrugged. "I think so, too, but I wear them anyway. Probably will until they fall apart."

"It's tough to let go, isn't it?" She smiled again, a smile that warmed him more than the seventy-degree morning. "I'm Rosie Duvall."

Rosie. He liked her name. It fit her.

"Sam," he said, "Sam Johnson." He paused, gathering his courage. Avoiding looking at her, he asked, "Would you like to go sit on the bench under the mulberry tree with me? Maybe visit a little?"

She was quiet a second. Had he asked for her company too soon? Did she think him some kind of old weirdo out to pick up women in the park? His stomach knotted.

Then, one slight, thin-boned hand settled on his arm. He studied her and saw her smile grow larger.

"I've been waiting for weeks for you to ask," Rosie said. "I came here today hoping to see you, planning to talk to you."

Feeling younger than he had in years, Sam patted her hand. Her skin felt like velvet. He'd missed the touch of another person. His legs were no longer tired. His heart didn't feel as heavy. She came here hoping to see me. He liked hearing that.

"I call it my 'wishing tree.' You probably think that's foolish." He wouldn't tell her how many wishes to have his sweet wife back he'd made there.

She shook her head, the sun dancing on her silver hair. "I call it my 'remembering tree.' It's where I look back on all the good times in my life. And acknowledge that I want to have more good times."

He was glad he'd come to the park. He'd almost stayed home, but something made him feel like he had to walk here today, even if his energy level had been a little down.

Sam tucked her small hand in the crook of his arm. "Well, let's go share some memories."

A BLINK OF AN EYE

Annie stood in front of the bathroom mirror in her hotel room. Who was that woman with the short, multi-shaded brown hair, with gray teasing the roots? She stared down at her hands, again disconcerted by the whisper thin lines and the half dozen small brown spots. When had that happened? At least when she turned her hands over and glanced at her palms, they appeared the same as always.

Her cell phone rang and she dashed into the main room, snagging the phone before it would go to voicemail. She recognized her daughter's caller ID. "I made it here okay," she said in reassurance. "Only a slight delay at the airport getting my bag."

"If you would carry it on like I suggested it," Faith said with a hint of amusement. They discussed the matter every time Annie flew, both knew she preferred to check her bag and would not change that decision. "You're so stubborn, Mom."

"I get it from you."

Faith laughed. "It works the other way around, remember." She listened to two of her children yelling at each other in the background over some TV show. "Before I go take charge of that problem, are you going to make it to your afternoon Meet and Greet?"

Annie sat down on the side of the bed and pulled in a deep, steadying breath. Time had jumped forward in a blink of an eye. She would attend her first high school graduation reunion today. She sucked in another deep breath, held it for a few counts before releasing it.

"You're doing those deep breathing exercises again, aren't you?"

"Maybe," Annie said. "Oh, all right, yes." She glanced at herself in the mirror above the dresser across from her. There was that aging woman again, one she hardly recognized. "I'm too old for this nonsense of attending a high school reunion. I've never attended one before. Why did I decide to come this time?"

Faith snorted her disagreement. "Sixty-eight isn't too old for anything. Besides, this is special, your 50th reunion."

"But none of the high school friends I have kept in touch with plan to come. They don't understand why I'm bothering with it." And she hadn't had a good answer for them.

"What was I thinking? The hotel and flight reservations from San Antonio to Wichita, plus the rental car from there to Compton for this weekend is an extravagance. I could better use the money for replacing the outdated kitchen counters. Or going on a Caribbean cruise with my travel friends. Or ... Well, for many other things."

Faith huffed her disapproval. "You can afford all of those things plus this weekend. Stop stalling. You're there because you kept telling me that something was drawing you there. Go find out what that something is."

Her daughter was right. A gut instinct had insisted this was important and wouldn't let her ignore it. Although sometimes her gut instinct had let her down. Her ex-husband a sterling example of that. She'd believed Wes Laughlin would be her knight in shining armor, her one true love forever. Except his "armor" had been rusty. His "love" fading more with each passing year until he'd hit a mid-life crisis where he'd changed from the man she'd married. Then he'd hit a sixty-five-crisis and developed the need to search out other beds, other women. At least he'd given her Faith, the daughter she loved so much.

She shoved thoughts of the rotten rat she'd divorced three years ago aside. Her life was more than fine without him. She could do what she wanted when she wanted. He'd told Faith that her mother was being foolish about this reunion matter, wasting her retirement money and her time. It was really some of her settlement money from him, which made the trip all the more enjoyable.

Despite Annie's issues with him, Faith maintained a relationship with her father. A strained one. She smiled at the memory of her daughter relating how she'd told him, "Her money, her time. None of your business, Dad."

Okay, she was here in her hometown. She darn well planned to attend the reunion. "Better get going if I'm going to discover what pulled me here this weekend."

"Phone me later."

When the call ended, Annie peered back at the mirror. Enough fretting about the changes in her face, the gray in her hair, even the few extra pounds she carried. Standing, she decided the new navy-blue blouse and tan slacks she'd purchased the other day looked acceptable and stylish. The blue set off her eyes, looked good with the tan gained from all those hours laboring in her gardens. As she shifted away, she caught the reflection of the 18-year-old girl she remembered. Sometimes we saw what we preferred to see.

Time to get moving. The Meet and Greet session scheduled to lead off the weekend's reunion events would begin soon in the hotel's dining room.

******

Gary couldn't believe he was here in his hometown. He didn't understand why he'd come today. High school hadn't been the best time in his life. He'd struggled with his friends, his family... and with girlfriends. Over the last five decades, he'd shunted most of that to the back of his mind. Most.

He flicked off the TV in his hotel room and his thoughts wandered again. There had been one girl he'd wondered about more than once over the years. She'd had curly, wild brown hair often pulled back into a ponytail to control it. Blue eyes, serious eyes, shy eyes. He and Annie hadn't gone out all that long for stupid reasons. The memory of her popped into his thoughts at odd times, like now. He'd liked her laugh and how smart she'd been. Too smart for a jock like him. Had she ever thought of him?

He groaned. What the heck was he doing? He was a man of the moment. Not a dweller on the past. He never dragged out photo albums his mother had insisted on making for him, never looked at old yearbooks. So, what was he doing here?

Disgusted with over-thinking the situation, he snatched his room key off the small desk. This was a waste of his time, his money, too. The money wasn't an issue for him but his time was valuable.

Okay, he'd go to the opening get-together because he needed to eat. Then he'd check out of the hotel and drive back to Kansas City. His business partners had wanted a projection meeting this weekend. It had displeased them he had put it off for this reunion. They would love for him to change his mind.

As he closed the door, a familiar emptiness filled him. True, his partners would like that. Otherwise he would return to his massive, empty house. Pamela wouldn't be there to welcome him home. She'd raised their kids, played hostess for him and his business for many years. A year ago, she'd decided she wanted something more. A life of her own. It hadn't been difficult to let her go. They'd drifted apart during their almost 40 years of marriage. He didn't miss her, just the companionship. There had been little of that. Each of them went their separate ways. Besides their grown children they had nothing in common. They liked different books, movies, restaurants, politics, and just about everything. Had they ever liked the same things?

He thrust the troubling thoughts aside. Enough of that pity-party crap. He had a substantial, prosperous Internet security business. His house was in the finest neighborhood and he had three cars he enjoyed... all that could go a little too fast sometimes. Plus, there was his extravagant hunting cabin in Colorado that he'd bought a dozen years ago to get away from Pamela and the frustrations at home. Except he couldn't remember the last time he'd gone there. Work consumed him. He could retire but then what would he do?

******

Laughing at one of her acquaintance's observations about her twin granddaughters playing T-ball, Annie peered around the packed hotel meeting room. She didn't recognize ninety percent of her old classmates. They shared nothing beyond being in her high school class. She doubted she would see any of them again.

"Carrie was the one who hit the ball," Barbara-something said. "But Cassie hopped off the bench and both girls ran to first base." She howled and snagged a lot of attention from people visiting at other high-topped tables. "As did the other seven girls who also had been on the bench. It was hilarious!"

Annie smiled. The description brought back memories of watching her grandsons play T-ball. A crazy time in the beginning phases of playing ball for the coaches.

As her gaze veered toward the room's entrance, she blinked in surprise. Now that was someone she wouldn't have expected to see here. Taller than she recalled and broader through the shoulders, Gary Thorndale stood staring at the throng of classmates. His black hair remained as thick as ever, cut and styled. Silver threaded through it making him look distinguished, appealing. He'd aged well. Why did men seem to improve with age? Well, some men. Her ex-husband had rounded out and wore a weird comb-over to hide his balding head. He'd turned into what her friends had called a Butterball turkey, emphasis on "turkey."

She flashed back to the moment, realizing she had been staring at Gary for far too long. He wouldn't recognize her. They'd only dated a few months in their junior year. Not that she'd forgotten him. She still had the long-ago squashed remnants of the corsage he'd given her for the prom. She kept silly mementos like that.

"Isn't that Gary... something? I can't remember his last name," her temporary friend said, her gaze fixated across the room. "Didn't he go to some Texas college on a football scholarship? Everyone assumed he would go pro, but... Something happened that I can't recall."

"Texas A&M," Annie explained as the other woman raised an eyebrow in curiosity. "He screwed up his knee."

Okay, she'd followed his life for a few years after high school. She'd liked him a lot but she hadn't been enough for him. Their junior prom date had been a "pity date," arranged by their mothers. Their dating time after that awkward. She was a dreamy-eyed teenage girl elated to be with the popular quarterback. He'd just tried to please his mother by being nice to timid, quiet Annie for a while.

"Annie? Annie Golden?" a rich voice fortified with a slight Texas drawl said as the center of her thoughts stepped closer.

Her heart pounded just like that silly teenage girl. She drew in a steadying breath and faced the man towering over her. "Annie Laughlin," she corrected. She'd kept her ex's name because it was just too complicated to change it.

Deep dimples she remembered emerged around Gary's smile. It reached his brown eyes and laugh lines etched their corners. "Right. You married Wes Laughlin in college." He chuckled at her obvious surprise. "Mom kept me informed about anything here in our hometown and about her friends. At least she did for a while."

"Mine did too." The admission hurt.

Her mother had died ten years ago, but until that time she'd kept Annie up to date on everyone and everything in and from Compton. Including Gary's success in the business world and about his marriage to some Dallas socialite. Neither of their mothers had approved of his bride choice. They hadn't liked her choice of a husband either. She'd read about his recent divorce in the updates about their high school class. How or why that had gotten included was beyond her understanding. But they had failed marriages in common. That was all. She wasn't in his social class. He was a key player in a major Internet security consulting firm with offices in Dallas and Kansas City, had a national reputation as a business whiz. She was a retired social worker. A world of difference.

He cleared his throat, sounding almost nervous, and got her attention again. "Would you walk with me around the downtown area? We can check out the changes firsthand."

His suggestion appealed to her but she should decline. She should stay here and visit with her temporary friend. But...

Gary's smile faded and he glanced around the room filled with virtual strangers. "Never mind. It was a silly idea."

He angled away. "I'll let you get back to talking with your friend." He glanced back. "I had decided to just grab something to eat and leave.

Coming here was a mistake."

"No!" Annie reached out to grasp his forearm. "You came all this way, don't go yet." She felt foolish, but she didn't want him to leave.

When he glanced down at her hold on his arm, she released him, embarrassed. "Sorry."

"I'm not." His smile returned, making him even more handsome.

Before she could stop herself, she blurted, "I'd love to go walk around with you. Catch up."

"Good." He studied her for a second. "You look the same. Same brown hair; a few more highlights. Maybe it isn't as bouncy as I remember. And the same beautiful blue eyes."

Annie gave him an "are you serious?" look. "You need glasses." She fingered her shoulder-length hair, much shorter than when he would have last seen her. "Those highlights you mentioned are there to hide the gray. And I have my hair straightened these days." He remembered those wild curls? The idea warmed her.

He shrugged, emphasizing his broad shoulders again. "Got gray myself." He helped her off the high stool, nodding at her tablemate. "You don't mind if I take Annie away, do you?"

The woman waved them off. "Not at all. Go argue about gray hair."

Gary settled Annie's hand in the bend of his arm and her heart fluttered in excitement. Just as it had the so long-ago day he'd presented her with the corsage. His hands had been shaking and her mother had had to pin it on her dress. But he didn't look uneasy now. He looked... pleased. To see her.

She laughed self-consciously. "I hadn't planned to come this weekend. Something just... Well, something called me here." She glanced at him. "Sounds ridiculous, doesn't it?"

He chuckled, the sound full and deep. "Last-minute decision for me, too, to my business partners' frustration." He turned serious. "I don't do that often. This time it was a good decision because I ran into you."

Because I'm here? Wow! Not that anything more than renewing an old friendship would come of this chance meeting. "We both made good decisions."

He put a hand on top of hers and squeezed. Looking sheepish, he asked, "Do you remember that half-wilted corsage I brought you for the junior prom?"

Annie nodded. She wouldn't tell him she still had it. He'd think her strange. "It wasn't 'half-wilted.'"

"Yes, it was." He lifted one eyebrow in challenge. "I'd about strangled it to death carrying it. I should have left it in the box but I didn't."

She giggled. "Maybe it was a little pathetic looking." Worse now.

"That's putting it kindly," Gary said with a chuckle.

He led her from the meeting room, down the hallway, and toward the outer door of the hotel. "Catch me up on your life," he cajoled as they walked. "Are you still living in Texas someplace? I think that was the last I heard from Mom."

"Yes, in the San Antonio area," she admitted. "But compared to yours, I've had a boring life." He was just making polite conversation, but it was nice.

"Not from what Mom has shared with me." He met her gaze, thoughtful. "I want to know."

She tingled all over like a teenage girl with a crush. The big, gorgeous quarterback was interested in her. No. The attractive older man seemed curious. Surreal.

He peered down the sidewalk and admitted in a cautious tone, "I've thought about you. Wondered if maybe you were the one who got away. As cliché as that sounds," he added under his breath.

"It does sound like a cliché but still nice." Again, she would never tell him she'd wondered about him, too. If they'd continued dating…

Uncomfortable with those musings, she went back to her life. A safe topic. "I'm a retired social worker." She glanced at him with a weak smile. "I warned you. I haven't made headlines or made a big splash in the business world like you."

He squeezed her hand again, giving her a gentle look. "Making headlines and splashing around are good. But I'm sure you've affected people's personal lives. That's important, Annie."

"But—"

"No 'buts' about it. Those people you've touched and helped over the years will remember you." He furrowed his brow and took a second before continuing. "I keep businesses safe in the Internet world. But my company's importance in their lives is momentary."

Annie supposed that was true. And she still had people she'd worked with and befriended keep in contact with her. "Thanks for reminding me about that. I've been suffering minor depression about no longer working in the community. Feeling restless, I guess."

"A life change like retirement is quite an adjustment."

"Planning on making more headlines and splashing around a while longer, aren't you?" It was odd how relaxed she felt strolling with him, talking.

"When I go to that next step, will you give me pointers on adjusting?" He stopped to consider her with a serious expression. "Work is what I do, who I am. I'll have an identity crisis."

She met his troubled gaze and nodded in empathy. "Been there, still working through my crisis."

She had experienced a sense of confusion for several months after she'd stopped working. Without having to report in every day, she had struggled to find her footing again. She'd continued waking up early without a reason to do so. She'd felt useless for a while.

"It hasn't been easy," she said on a sigh.

"I'm sure it hasn't. But I feel you're about done adjusting." He hauled in a breath. "Tell no one—not my kids or my partners but retiring scares the hell out of me."

His worried eyes told her what he said was true. Retirement worried him. "It's not as scary as it seems at first. You'll be fine. After you learn to be okay with your changes."

He didn't appear convinced and she lightened the moment. "I had a rude awakening this morning when I looked in the mirror. There was this old lady with age lines on her face and gray at her hair roots. The sight startled me."

"That's not who I see."

She laughed. "Me either, most of the time. My mind's eye still sees the eighteen-year-old girl with her life ahead of her. Fresh faced. Eager for each new day." She laughed again, blushing. "That girl is part of me but not who I am now. It's time to accept the new me."

"I remember the younger you." He smiled, reaching up to stroke her cheek. "She was pretty. You're beautiful. From the inside out."

Annie sniffed. "You don't even know me."

"No, I don't know who you are today. The girl I remember from high school was quiet, kind, and smart." He grinned. "Mom must have told me a hundred times I screwed up when we stopped dating."

He'd seen her as kind? Interesting. "I wasn't what you wanted in a girlfriend. Not flirty enough. Not pretty enough. Not..." She stopped, exasperated that she'd confessed her past hurts.

"Annie, I was a seventeen-year-old jock. Girls threw themselves at me and I didn't resist." Again, he touched her cheek. "You were always pretty enough. I was just... stupid."

"Yes, you were." She grinned. His admission went a long way toward healing those old bruises to her heart.

He chuckled, then he sobered. "Think we could try again?"

She blinked. "What?"

"I'd like to get to know the 'new' Annie. See if you'd like anything about the jock who grew up. Maybe even spend time with him."

Wow! Maybe she was still being that silly teenage girl who had a crush on Gary Thorndale. How could anything work between them when they lived in different cities? When their lives were so dissimilar?

Oh, what the heck! "How about we start with sharing coffee and a piece of pie at Dayton's Diner? Remember that place? It's still there."

Pleasure warmed his eyes. "Apple, with lots of ice cream on top?"

She tucked her hand in his and tugged him down the sidewalk. "I claim the first bite."

He laughed again and she felt better than she had in a while. It felt like time had slid back fifty years… in the blink of an eye.

TAKING THAT FIRST STEP

"Are you listening, Mom?"

Daisy O'Brien stood on the porch of her cabin and sighed at her oldest son's question. "Of course." Not really.

"No, you weren't."

"Okay, guilty as charged." She wished she could toss her cell phone down, stomp on it. Maybe throw it in the nearby lake.

This would be a conversation she didn't want to have. Again. She'd much rather focus on nature's beauty around her. The early fall day couldn't be prettier. Burnished golds, oranges, and even reds tinged the leaves of the maples, elms, Bradford Pears, and willows. A light breeze, not too cool, flitted by and brought the smell of a fire in the large man-made pit at the center of the campground. She loved it all. Spring here was also magnificent, but fall was her favorite time of year.

Bob huffed in her ear, snagging her attention. "This is important." She could visualize the serious expression on his face: furrowed brow, brown eyes focused with determination, tight jaw. He needed to lighten up about life. Mentioning that to him never went well though.

"I've got a hundred things I should do right now." She knew the excuse wouldn't work, but at least she tried.

Her son wouldn't be easily dissuaded. "I've found someone interested in buying the campground. I don't think he will even try to negotiate the asking price."

"You are the one who doesn't listen, son." She counted to five, then ten under her breath.

"You're doing that counting thing, aren't you?"

"It calms me." She took a second before adding, "There is no 'asking price' to consider negotiating. Because I'm not ready to think about selling the camp."

She'd lived here forty years and couldn't imagine living anywhere else. They'd discussed this many times. Her four grown children— bless their hearts—thought they knew what was best for her now that she was a widow. It wasn't "being alone" out here in the country.

"I worry about you. We all worry about you being so isolated out there."

"I know, dear." She understood their concern, but she'd never felt isolated here. "There are neighbors who stop in to check on me. Even one of the county sheriffs drops by at least every other day."

She could tell by his grumbling that he didn't consider that enough. "You know I'm rarely alone. Camp O'Brien is so popular that I'm seldom without other people around." And she was cautious about who she allowed to come stay here, even for just a day or a weekend. She asked for references and checked them out. Nobody had ever balked at her requirement.

Daisy heard a mosquito whining and needed to end this call. Had she put out enough citronella candles in the conference building for today's group meeting? And around the fire pit area they would also use? Maybe she needed to bring out some bug spray too.

But her son wasn't giving up yet. "Mom, managing that campground is too much work for you."

"I'm fine. Really. I just need to find some new help with the various chores." The place required constant upkeep, and she needed at least part-time help. Not that she minded hard labor herself. It hadn't been bad when Daniel had been alive. They'd shared the chores and the many maintenance tasks, including care of the grounds.

"New help? What happened with Greg?"

Shoot. She wished he hadn't picked up on that slip. Now he'd worry even more. "He told me a few days ago that he can't keep working here on weekends. His college schedule is becoming too complicated. I'll put an ad in the newspaper next week."

He grumbled again. "Mom, you've got a valuable asset there. Something you can sell and be financially set for the rest of your life. You won't have to work so hard."

She and her husband had built a comfortable place for groups to come on retreats, families to come for brief vacations, even individuals wanting to spend a day away from the city. The camp's reputation had been hard earned and they had devoted customers. She was proud of the well-maintained cabins and conference facilities but they required work. The twenty-five acres that made up the campground also took a lot of time and energy. As much as she wished otherwise, she couldn't do it alone.

"I know you mean well but I'm not interested in selling right now. I wish you and the others would accept my decision." She loved Bob to death but as a successful real estate agent, he could sometimes try her patience.

Glancing at the log-cabin style conference building where twenty people gathered around the fire pit roasting marshmallows, she sighed in contentment. It always made her feel good to have visitors here enjoying themselves.

"There are some nice apartment complexes in Wichita for active seniors," he cajoled. "You could get involved in their activities. Just enjoy yourself. Not—"

Daisy cleared her throat to cut him off. "I've told you before, I'm not wild about living anywhere else." She pulled in a deep, calming breath. "My home is comfortable. I love the log house your dad and I built. The life we built."

Bob was breathing hard, probably fisting his hands as he often did, a habit from way back in his toddler years.

"It's a great house," he admitted. "But it's too big for you with all of us gone now."

Her home was much bigger than she needed but it was her home. Period. She intended to live here until she couldn't. "I can't imagine not getting up each morning and spending most of the day outside or working on this or that around the campground."

"So, you want me to back off. Again." He sounded resigned, not happy.

"Yes."

"You'll run that help wanted ad? Or do you want me to do it?"

"I can handle it, thanks." She would miss the college kid who worked here during the summer and on weekends but she understood his situation. Replacing him would be hard. Few people appreciated working out in the country. But she'd find someone. She had to think positive.

"Okay, I'll drop the property selling idea...for now." He hesitated. "Love you, Mom."

"Love you, too."

As she ended the call, Daisy spotted a man sitting on a log near the muddy lake. She'd noticed him when he first arrived and meandered over that way. She thought he'd been there ever since. A loner, she supposed, and wondered why he'd even come here with the group. But there was something about him that attracted her. She'd watched him from a distance earlier while cleaning up some scattered trash from a can that raccoons had got into last night.

Maybe she'd just go share a few minutes with him, make sure he was all right.

******

Bill Anderson sat on a thick, six-foot log beside the lake that looked as still as brown glass. Occasionally a fish broke the surface leaving behind a widening circle as it disappeared again into the murky depths. In the multi-colored trees and leafless elms along the opposite bank, a flock of starlings filled the otherwise peaceful country air with a chorus of bird song. He felt at peace for the first time in a while. He'd needed this day trip.

"Would you mind if I sit here, too?" came a soft feminine voice behind him. Footsteps moved over the crisp, fallen leaves. "This is such a nice viewing spot."

He tramped down the urge to say, "No, I'd prefer privacy." Instead he shifted to glance back at the sixty-something woman with blonde-gray hair somewhat hidden beneath a battered straw hat that boasted an enormous daisy on its brim. She sported an odd little crooked smile. He'd seen her arrive late to the Senior Adult Singles Retreat. A retreat he hadn't been interested in attending. She hadn't stayed long and he wasn't sure why she'd left. Maybe to have some alone time, like him.

He nodded toward the other end of the log. "Reckon I can share the space."

She beamed, the tiny wrinkles around her mouth deepening into dimples. "I'm Daisy. Daisy O'Brien." Tugging up her jeans, she eased down onto the log near him. "My hearing isn't what it used to be, so I need to sit close enough to catch what you say."

Considering he wore a pair of hearing aids himself, he understood. "Bill Anderson."

A squirrel that had been scurrying around searching for something in the lakeside brush darted in their direction. When he discovered the older couple, he screeched to a halt. He puffed out his cheeks before he scampered away, chattering in obvious annoyance.

"We've upset the little rascal," Daisy said, amusement dancing in her soft tone.

"He did appear irritated." He'd always liked watching squirrels, curious little creatures. Nuisances sometimes, too, like when they messed with his bird feeders.

"I suppose he's gathering up foodstuffs before winter."

Bill nodded. "Planning for the future."

He thought of all the plans he and his precious Alice had made years ago. They'd planned to move to a place in the country when he retired. His roots were from the country but he'd had to move into the city after he got out of the service and worked at one of the aircraft plants in Wichita to support his wife and baby. He'd always dreamed of leaving the fast-paced city life behind and settling some place where he'd have room for a large garden, space to breathe. It had never worked out for him and Alice, and now she'd been gone more than two years.

"Never make plans myself." Daisy laughed, and the light sound swirled around them. "That's how I ended up here," she patted her jeans, "wearing less than my best duds."

"You look fine."

"Oh, you're a charmer." She smiled again. "I'm wearing my old yard-working clothes but I don't care. Never was much on showing off for others."

"I'm not a 'charmer,' just honest." He felt himself blushing.

Daisy tipped her head back toward the common area in front of the row of cabins and conference center where the other camp guests were gathering. "Well, Priscilla Waverly, the coordinator for this retreat, sure looked down her long nose at me when I showed up earlier dressed this way."

He hadn't ever liked Priscilla Waverly. "She's the one looks odd here today, wearing that fancy pants outfit."

Daisy's musical laughter once more drifted around him. "She's my sister, although we've not much in common. We seldom even speak unless she wants something from me—like today."

The noise from the people behind them grew louder. Priscilla's high-pitched voice grated on Bill's nerves, another reason he'd walked away from the group. "What does she want from you?"

Daisy pointed to a flatbed loaded with hay bales and attached to a large, older model tractor. "To pull you all around on a hayrack ride."

Bill blinked, gawking at the slim, short woman. He couldn't imagine her driving that big metal monster.

"Been driving it for years." She grinned, as if she'd read his thoughts.

"I own O'Brien Camp. My dear Daniel and I bought it years ago although he never liked it out here. City boy but he understood that I wasn't meant for all that hustle and bustle—being an old farm girl. He loved me enough to put up with my country-loving ways. He was a good man."

Was. She's a widow, like me. "Didn't like this?" Bill glanced around. "How could anyone not like such a beautiful place?" Oh, the cabins could use a little work, and some junk piles needed to go. Everything else seemed perfect.

She shrugged a slender shoulder. "He didn't mind it but he didn't love it as much as I did either."

Bill was quiet a second. "I always wanted to live out in the country. Alice, my wife, was always too frail, so we needed to live close to hospitals. I'd be content in a place like this. Room for taking long walks, spots for fishing."

******

A fish jumped and drew their attention as it splashed back into the murky water. Daisy saw the look of longing on Bill's still handsome face. He was bald on top, like Daniel had been. Did people tease Bill about it like they had her husband?

They sat quietly and she felt content beside this man. There was something amiable about him, something sad, too. Being a widow, she understood that. He'd been a good husband, giving up his dreams for what his wife had needed. Like Daniel had done, sort of. She perceived that Bill was struggling with his life now just as she was. Maybe he needed a change. Maybe…

"You interested in a job?" She held her breath, wondering how she could have just blurted out the question. Yet she didn't want to take the offer back. What would he think of a crazy woman like her being so bold like that?

He glanced at her, his eyes widening in surprise. "Are you offering me, an old man long past my prime, a job?"

Daisy rolled her eyes. "I'm well past my prime, too."

"Okay, neither of us is thirty anymore." He looked uneasy for a second and then asked, "Were you serious? About the job?"

Was she? She didn't know this man, hadn't checked his references. He'd come here with her sister's church group. So, she figured that was good enough, Besides, she considered herself a good judge of character.

She nodded. "Yes. I'm offering you a chance to enjoy country contentment and do odd jobs at the same time. You game?" Her kids, especially Bob, would have a fit. Tough. She would take a chance and she was sure this man needed to move on with his life.

"You don't know me." He scanned the surrounding area and she saw such longing in his expression.

"You don't know me either." She drew his focus once more. "But I have a good sense about people. I think we might work well together."

******

Did he dare? Bill wanted to jump at the opportunity but was he being a foolish old man?

"There's a caretaker's cabin just beyond the head of the lake over there." She pointed to their right. "You could live there at no charge as part of your payment for helping around here."

Tempting.

"Did I mention there are some of the biggest catfish you'll ever run across in Kansas in this lake?"

He thought about Alice, about the house they'd bought together and made into a home. How could he walk away from it, from all their memories there?

The memories will always be with you wherever you live. He heard the thought as though his beloved Alice had whispered it to him. It made sense. A house was just a building. The memories didn't dwell between frame walls; they lived in his mind, in his heart. He wanted to do this. Somehow, he'd figure out selling the house, a lot of the furniture. I could do it.

"Oh well, it was a silly idea, I suppose," Daisy said, sounding disappointed. She stood, the flower bobbing on the ridiculous hat.

He blinked back to the moment, realizing he'd taken too long to respond. He reached out to grasp her hand, taking the first step on the next part of his life. "Is next week too soon to move in?"

Her smile lit her eyes, and he knew everything would work out.

A QUILT FROM THE HEART

Marvin Thompson pulled his twenty-year-old Buick into a spot on the street across from the Havenville Senior Center. The old car's engine rumbled, the air conditioning worked sometimes, and the heater most of the time. He didn't care about any of those minor problems. No way would he trade it in for a newer model. His dear wife had picked out this car before she'd developed cancer, for the first time.

His eyes misted for a second and his old heart pinched. He pushed the sadness away and his stomach fluttered with nerves. Was the quilting class over yet? Could he go through with this? He was sweating bullets and it wasn't hot outside on this late spring day. This was a crazy idea.

As he turned off the car, it gave one final grumbling protest. "You should just forget it and go home," he said into the sudden silence. Nobody needed to know he'd even come up with this mission. Definitely not my kids. He could imagine what his daughter would think: that it was time he sold the house and moved in with she and her family. So she could watch after him.

Frustration spread through him. He wasn't ready to give up his home. Someday but not yet. He still needed the memories of Lula around him. And when he moved somewhere else, it wouldn't be into Hannah's home. As much as he loved her, her husband, and his three grandkids, that was a chaotic household he didn't need on a daily basis.

Thinking again about why he was here, he knew Lula would have called him a coward. He'd disappointed her so many times over the forty-two years of their marriage. She'd never told him so but he knew. He couldn't let her down again now that she was no longer with him.

His stepped out of the car and glanced toward the entrance to the center. A trio of older women walked out chattering away, carrying handled containers he assumed held their sewing supplies. His wife had used such containers when she'd gone to quilting sessions with her friends. One of her boxes sat in the backseat. Next to the plastic tub filled with squares for the last project she'd been working on.

As the women headed for their cars parked along the curb, he drew in four deep breaths. That was something his wife had taught him to do to calm his blood pressure down. He still did it when feeling anxious. Two more deep breaths and he felt calmer. Time to focus on the reason he'd come here. Dang it, he intended to follow through with this mission. The worst that could happen was the quilting instructor would turn him away in refusal.

******

Ellie Stewart handed the center's receptionist the check-in sheet for her class. Her usual three ladies had shown up for the gab session/ quilting time. They'd been getting together bi-weekly for more than three years now. Sometimes, a couple more experienced quilters showed up, sometimes, it would be only her and one other lady. She didn't care how many people came to her class. Coming here broke up her days of humdrum housecleaning, tending to her much too large herb garden, or watching TV. Her life had become B.O.R.I.N.G.

"You have a good afternoon, Alma," she said, turning toward the front door.

The middle-aged, African-American woman that she'd known for years gave her a smile. "Got any special plans today?"

"I've got a honeysuckle bush threatening to take over the world. I believe we'll battle it out today." She glanced back, laughing. "I am hoping to win." It was always a temporary win though.

"I'll be pulling for you." Alma chuckled and then her gaze darted to the door. "Oh dear, it looks like someone needs help to get in."

Before Alma could get out of her chair, Ellie shook her head. "I've got it." She hustled to the glass double doors.

A lanky and lean, silver-haired man stood holding a good-sized tub and trying to figure out how to open a door. His brow pinched in annoyance, he started to set the tub down.

Ellie shoved the main door open. "Don't bother doing that. I've got the door." She stepped out of the way to hold it back for him.

He peered at her, brow furrowing for an instant. His brown eyes flickered in surprise. "Ellie Stewart? Right?"

She nodded and studied him, then said, "Marvin? Marvin Thompson?" She'd met him a few times in the past, when his wife was a fellow member of the quilt guild. Then she remembered that Lula had passed on five years ago. What was he doing here? With a tub of fabric?

"You're who I came to see."

"Me?" She glanced at the tub he held. "Are you donating fabric to the quilters here? We can always use it."

"Not exactly." He walked past her to the big, round table in the corner of the visiting area. He sat the tub down as she followed him, curious.

He faced her and looked apprehensive. "I'm not donating anything. I came to ask for your help." He said the last in a near whisper.

She couldn't imagine what she could help him with, but she'd do whatever she could. "You've got my attention. What do you need?"

Heat inched up his neck, and he had trouble meeting her eyes. "I've got a bunch of quilt squares that Lula had worked on before..." He swallowed hard. "Before she died."

Ellie's compassion went out to him. She knew how close he and Lula had been. They'd adored each other. They'd married right out of high school, raised three kids, and planned to travel the world after he'd retired. Lula's health issues had flared up as so often did for retirees with plans. She'd fought cancer a couple of times. The last time had been her hardest battle, which she hadn't won.

Behind her, she heard Alma's quiet sympathetic sigh. His wasn't an unusual story around senior centers, except that more often than not it was the husband who died first. As in Ellie's case. Phillip left her a widow a dozen years ago and she still missed him.

She stepped closer to the tub, knowing she'd find some superbly put together squares inside. Lula had been a master quilter. "Do you want someone to turn them into a quilt for you? Find a place to donate the pieces? What?"

He cleared his throat. "I want you to teach me to quilt."

******

Marvin watched Ellie's eyes widen in surprise, as he'd expected. He heard the receptionist gasp. Yes, this was an unusual idea. But he would suck it up and do this.

He set a hand on the tub, sensing that his Lula was observing him and listening. It made him more determined.

"You know my Lula made quilts for all our kids and grandkids. A lot of them she put in those quilt shows here in town. Like that wedding ring quilt she made for our daughter, Hannah. And the crazy quilt she made for our daughter-in-law."

He thought about the hours and hours Lula spent in her sewing room. He'd spent a lot of time in his garage workshop. They'd both had their hobbies. She'd loved every second of quilting, though she sometimes grumbled a quiet colorful comment when something went wrong. He did much the same thing when one of his wood carving projects took a minor change from his plan.

Ellie smiled and it reached her grass green eyes. He knew she'd been a widow a long time. They had that in common. Beyond that, he'd always considered her a generous and friendly soul. Lula had too.

"I could make this quilt for you," she offered in a kind tone.

Her gentleness in this unique situation discomfited him. He studied the much shorter woman, rounded in the right places. For being in her early seventies, she was a handsome woman. Not as lovely as Lula but close. Lula had been perfect in his eyes.

He shifted feeling uncomfortable. Why was he thinking like that? Sure, he was lonely sometimes, missing female companionship. That wasn't why he'd come here today.

"I appreciate your offer but I want to do this myself." He glanced at the tub and removed the lid, lifting out two squares. He laid them on the table, feeling a tug at his heart.

Ellie inched beside him, touching first one square and then the other. "Lula always did such splendid handwork on her squares before she fastened them together on her machine."

"Yes." He struggled for two seconds as Ellie waited. "This quilt was to be for us. Not for one of our kids. Well... until someday."

She fingered one square, inspected it. "I recognize this material." She pointed to a triangle-shaped piece of a pink floral print. "It's from one of her favorite dresses, isn't it? Lula always looked so nice in it."

Marvin, too, remembered the dress. "She bought it special for our oldest daughter's college graduation." After that she'd worn it for anything she considered special.

He pointed to a square-shaped piece of yellow-checked print. "She made matching aprons for herself and our daughter out of this." He was sure Hannah still had her apron.

When he glanced at Ellie, she was blinking, her eyes sparkling with unshed tears. He felt like that, too. But he was manning up to keep in control.

Ellie picked up the other square, grinned up at him. "Your shirts, right?" With a laugh, she pointed at a circle shape cut from a wild Hawaiian print with flowers and flamingos. "From your trip to Maui?"

He nodded, his face warming. "Only place I ever wore that shirt. Not my style."

She giggled, gazing at his green Polo-style shirt. "But you wore it for Lula. And I bet you didn't even complain too much."

He shrugged. "A man's got to do, what a man's got to do." He'd done almost anything his wife had asked of him. Almost anything.

"So, will you help me?" He circled back to his reason for being here. "Teach me how to pull these squares together into something that won't be ridiculous? Show me how to use her quilting machine?"

******

Ellie didn't even have to consider her answer. "Absolutely!"

His shoulders relaxed in relief. Had he thought she would turn him down? No way. She found the idea charming that he wanted to tackle something so foreign to him because this had been important to his wife. She doubted Phillip would have been this daring. He would have boxed up everything and donated it to Goodwill or somewhere.

"I've been thinking about this for months. Wondering if I should even try it." He looked at his feet, uncomfortable. "At first, it was painful to even set foot in Lula's sewing room. My daughter and daughters-in-law wanted to pack all her sewing stuff and fabrics up and take it away. But I couldn't let them. Doing that felt wrong."

Darn him. Ellie blinked back tears threatening again. "You're a good man, Marvin Thompson."

"I try to be." He gave her a crooked smile, his age lines almost disappearing. "But a time or two Lula thought I needed improvement."

"Don't all men need improvement, according to their wives?" Ellie teased, feeling comfortable with him. "My Phillip did now and then." She grew thoughtful. "Perfect or not, I loved that man. But I'm moving on with life."

Marvin looked chagrined. "It's taken me a while longer than it should have but I'm trying to do that, too."

She patted his arm. "We grieve in our own way, in our own time."

He was quiet a second, then put the squares back in the tub. Without looking at her, he asked, "Would you have time to get coffee, maybe get an early meal?" He glanced her way and said in a nervous rush, "So we can talk about this project."

His uncertainty was endearing. She'd missed talking to a man for longer than a "Thank you" when they held the door open for her.

"Howard's Café sound okay? It's close to here." She set the lid on the tub and gave him a smile of encouragement.

That crooked grin was back. "Perfect."

******

The deadly sharp quilting pin missed where Marvin intended it to go and stabbed his index finger. Again. He winced. He'd never suspected quilting would be such a painful hobby. A drop of blood landed on the quilt square he was trying to pin to a row of other squares. He grumbled, "Got any more of that stain removal stuff?"

You'd think he would get better at this after two weeks of daily— except for weekends—sessions with Ellie and the other quilting ladies. Not so. They had taken him on as a group project. Maybe their home lives were so dull they needed time here with him. He'd become their source of amusement, something that rankled.

From across the classroom in the senior center, Ellie flashed him a sympathetic look. She sat next to a first-time visitor to the group, a newbie quilter like him. Ellie could qualify for sainthood in his opinion. Patient, no matter what disaster he'd created. He was becoming an expert with the seam ripper.

"Connie, can you get the stick for him?" Ellie asked. "Dorothy, see if he needs another Band-aid."

He would rather have had Ellie alone helping him. While she might laugh inwardly at his mistakes, the other ladies weren't as reserved. They snickered. His ego was taking a beating, yet he'd grown to like them all. He toughed it up.

Connie appeared at his side with the now familiar Spray'n Wash Pre-Treat Stain Stick. "Well, it doesn't look as bad as the last time." She took the fabric from him and put it on the table next to his sewing machine. With the ease of experience, she swiped it over the small stain. "Do you want me to go wash this in the bathroom sink? Or will you take care of it at home?"

The time for today's session, the last for the week, was about up and he was more than ready for that. He glanced toward Ellie. After that first time getting coffee and a meal together, they'd become dining buddies. They met some place different each time for an early meal after these work sessions. Neither of them liked to cook. And they both liked trying new places that weren't too expensive, playing at being food critics. It made them laugh. But he was gaining a few pounds. Still...

"We'll take care of it later." Ellie answered his unspoken question about if they were going out again today. She winked at him.

That teasing wink and simple smile warmed him. He looked up at Connie with a foolish grin. "What the boss said. I'll deal with it later."

Dorothy walked up with a bandage, eyes twinkling. "I believe the boss said, 'we'll take care of it later.'"

Ellie giggled and went back to helping the quilting newbie with her current problem.

Connie and Dorothy shared an amused look, snickering.

Okay, they were having fun at his expense. They must see he and Ellie as more than just quilting friends, eating buddies. Were they? Maybe. He hadn't given the idea any thought. She was easy to be with, made him smile, made him feel less lonely. He hoped he helped her too.

The thoughts unnerved him. He'd started this whole thing with the sole purpose of honoring Lula, finishing the quilt she'd wanted to be special. Getting involved with another woman had never entered his mind. As he gathered up his sewing supplies and put his sewing machine back in its travel bag, he worried about matters. He was so lost in his troubled musings that he didn't notice Connie, Dorothy, and the newbie leave the room. The room was just quiet.

He stood staring down at his tub and bag, confused. Should he tell Ellie he had plans and he couldn't go out to eat with her today? Should he ease back from whatever was developing between them?

The soft scent of the rose hand lotion Ellie used caught his attention. She stepped next to him and he tensed before looking at her. He was tongue-tied.

Her gaze was gentle as she looked up at him. "Why don't I take your quilt strip home with me? I can wash it and bring it back next week."

Somehow, she'd sensed his discomfort and was trying to help him. She always put others first, always offered what she felt they needed. That annoyed him. What about her wants and needs? He knew she was as lonely in her home as he was in his. She'd told him so, not harped on the subject, just mentioned it. They filled a hole in each other's lives. There was nothing wrong with that. Maybe nothing more would ever come of this friendship. Did that matter? No.

"I'll let you wash that strip, since you offered. You're better at it than I am." It was the truth. This wasn't his first blood stain problem. He'd destroyed the first square he'd stained and tried to wash. She'd saved him on the next damaged square.

"Sure," she agreed, sounding disappointed. She reached for the folded-up strip but he stopped her, making her look at him again.

"How about checking out that new Cracker Barrel?" Nerves tangled inside him. He hoped he hadn't screwed up by seeming reluctant about going out today.

Her beautiful smile returned. "Shall we drive together this time?"

Usually they both drove, which was silly. If he picked her up at her house, would this qualify as a date? Would that be so terrible?

"It's a date." He blinked in surprise. "I...I..."

"We don't have to put a label to what we're doing, Marvin."

He heaved a sigh. "You must think me an idiot."

She shook her head. "Not at all." Her cheeks grew pink. "I've gone out a few times since Phillip died so long ago. But I've never felt as comfortable with another man as I do with you."

He liked that idea although he wouldn't tell her. But he admitted, "I haven't dated in over forty-five years. Even back then I wasn't good at it. Lula just...she made it easy."

Ellie gave him that sweet smile he liked so much. "I'll try to make it easy on you, too."

"I'd appreciate that."

Together they gathered his sewing stuff. She pulled the sewing machine bag and he carried the small plastic tub. Moving on. He realized as they walked outside together that he was moving on with his life. All because of his determination to complete the quilt his beloved Lula had started.

MAKING NEW MEMORIES

"Mom, this isn't a good idea."

Kate glanced at her thirty-six-year-old daughter standing beside her in Liz's driveway. If they reversed the situation, she would feel the same protective way. When you loved someone, you worried. Still, this was her life, her bucket list. She'd done the appropriate and safe thing most of her life. "Most" being a keyword. Forty years ago… She didn't wish to go there. Nobody was perfect.

"I'll be just fine."

She squared her shoulders and took the keys to her son-in-law's orange Jeep that she was borrowing for two days. Her pulse galloped in excitement. The mid-May day was flawless with blue skies, the temperature not too hot or too cool. Ready for the adventure, she said, "I need to get going. After I check into the hotel, I want to drive around the area."

The daughter she loved with all her heart continued to look unsettled. Beneath the sweep of blond hair across her forehead, her brow furrowed. Blue eyes so like Kate's mirrored concern. "I should take two days off work. I—"

"Unnecessary," Kate cut her off, knowing her daughter had several important meetings this week. She opened the Jeep's door and prepared herself for climbing up into it, stretching as high as she could. Made for off-roading, it had extra-large wheels and sat higher than most Jeeps. She was a tall woman and could handle this minor inconvenience. Besides, driving it made her feel bad ass.

By the time she settled behind the steering wheel, she felt proud of herself. She grinned as she peered down at her daughter. "Stop worrying about me. I can do this."

Liz nibbled her lower lip for a second and then released it on a sigh. "You're right, Mom. I don't know why I'm trying to change your mind. We're both headstrong women. When we decide on something, we're not easily swayed from the decision."

"Your dad called me 'stubborn to the extreme.' Not true. I gave in… sometimes." When she concluded that he was right.

"Like mother, like daughter." Liz laughed and then grew serious again. "We've talked about wanting to go hot air ballooning." Her eyes hinted at regret. "I wish we were doing it together. I hate to think of you having this experience alone."

Kate pulled the door closed and lowered the window. The action had her recalling the many other trips they'd gone on together. Driving across Scotland, searching for Loch Ness and missing it on the first try. Staying in the supposedly-haunted hunting lodge in Wales. So many other adventures. She missed those times. But life had changed for her precious daughter, her travel companion. Now there was Liz's husband to consider. Not that she resented him. Oh, no, she was happy for them both. Still, times with her daughter were forever different.

She shoved that second of melancholy aside. Not going there! Happy for them, remember? Now I have a daughter and a son to love.

"Mom, are you okay?" Liz broke into her musings.

"Of course, just…" Kate didn't finish the thought. She didn't want to tell her daughter where her mind had wandered. She drew in a breath, smiled as she blew it out. "When I visit you, there are always so many things to do. Piddle around in your gardens. Play in your pool. Barbecue. Go shopping. We never go to Napa Valley."

Liz looked crestfallen. "I'm sorry. I've let you down."

Kate hated that she'd made Liz feel bad. "No, you haven't. I enjoy everything we do together."

She adjusted the rearview mirror and checked the side mirrors, trying to come up with words to make up for upsetting her daughter. "I can experience this on my own." She met Liz's uncertain gaze. "Besides, I won't be alone. The tour is sold out. There'll be sixteen of us in the balloon."

Liz stepped back, "Without these client meetings, I would go with you. You know that, right?" Disappointment tinged her voice.

Kate nodded. She would very much have enjoyed sharing this adventure with her daughter. Sometimes life got in the way though. Life, other meaningful relationships, and work responsibilities. She swallowed down her own disappointment.

"I'll take lots of pictures. I'll fill up all of my phone's memory with them." She laughed, trying to lighten the moment. "Tomorrow night we can look at them. I'll bore you to death, I promise."

Liz's expression eased, and she chuckled. "That's something I can count on." She moved further back on the driveway. "Call me when you get to the hotel."

With a bob of her head, Kate backed into the street. Again, excitement spread through her. She'd wanted to ride in a hot-air balloon since she was a little girl and first saw them gliding across the sky. As she'd aged, she'd hoped to share the adventure with someone close to her, her daughter or her own husband.

Her heart hurt as she drove away. Liz couldn't fit it into her schedule on Kate's visits here. She was okay with that. And her husband—God bless him—had passed away three years and five months ago, almost to this day. Nick would want her to keep on doing things, work on checking off more items on the bucket list they'd prepared together.

A tear slid down her cheek and she swiped it away. She would miss him until her dying day, remember all their special moments together. It wasn't like she wasted a lot of time wallowing in grief over her loss. Not her style. Instead, she felt blessed about the years they'd had together. She kept busy as she had always done. He'd never tried to smother her by demanding that they spend all of their time together. They'd had their own interests, their personal friends. But they'd also enjoyed each other and their families. They went places together, had their favored restaurants. Some of her favorite times, though, had been just sitting together watching TV. Okay, arguing about what to watch on TV.

Good memories, all. Now she focused on making new memories. She believed every day was a gift. She planned to enjoy each one.

Kate had to admit that she preferred sharing experiences with others. Like the photos she planned to take tomorrow. She would sit with Liz and they'd look at them all. Still, sharing the actual moment of the experience with someone was different.

She peeked at the GPS map on the Jeep's dashboard screen that her daughter had set for her. Paper maps were a thing of the past. Although sometimes technically-challenged, she was getting better at following these computerized directions. And she'd learned to laugh at the annoyed voice that often said, "Recalculating" when she missed a turn.

As she swung onto the road that would take her to the highway, she wondered if she would meet someone today who would share the adventure with her. That would sure be nice. A new friend for a few hours.

******

"Are you sure about this, Dad? If you'd stick around until the weekend, I could go with you."

Joe shook his head, settling into the driver's seat of the Toyota sedan he was borrowing. Troy didn't think his older truck could make the trip to Napa Valley. His son was wrong but he'd humored him.

"There's no need to wait. You're busy with your family on weekends." The instant his son's brow furrowed he regretted adding that last part. "As you should be," he said and meant it. He'd been busy every weekend for a lot of years with his own kids.

Guilt seemed to weigh on Troy's shoulders, making them slump beneath his suit jacket "But I—"

"Don't worry about it. I understand." Joe pulled sunglasses from his shirt pocket. "I've decided on this and already made my reservations." He set the sunglasses in place on his nose. "Luck was with me on this sudden decision. I got the last spot on the balloon tour and the last hotel room."

Troy looked puzzled and not for the first time. "I don't get it. You've never talked about going ballooning before. Where did this idea come from?"

"From a California tourist magazine," Joe explained, a little surprised himself. He was more of a going-to-ballgames type of man, or playing a round of golf, or taking in a movie. He'd been waiting for his son in the community room of the senior living apartment complex the other night. Bored, he'd picked up the magazine and thumbed through it.

"The colorful ads for a balloon adventure company in Napa Valley caught my attention. I felt compelled to check out their website.

Then, almost before I knew what I was doing, I signed up for a tour."

"You've never been impulsive before, Dad. This isn't like you." Worry filled Troy's eyes.

It wasn't like him, his son was right. So much in Joe's life had changed since losing his wife four years ago. When he'd retired and sold his plumbing business back in Kansas, he'd moved closer to his son. The move had taken him months. But he'd been determined to do it. He liked being around Troy, his wife, and his two growing grandsons. Spending time with them didn't feel like enough though. Nor did hanging out with the other widowed men where he lived. Something was still missing from his life although he couldn't quite figure out what it could be.

"No sense in trying to figure out why I made this decision. I just did." Joe pushed down on the brake and then the button to start the engine, something still new to him. He missed the old ways of using an actual key. "It's time for you to head to the office. And I want to hit the road. I'll see you tomorrow night."

Troy breathed a sigh of acceptance and glanced at his watch. "You're right. I've got a big day ahead and my sons' ballgame to go to tonight." They played on the same team.

"Tell the boys I'm sorry about missing the game but I'll catch the next one." He supposed he should feel bad about missing tonight's game. Instead, anticipation spread through him. He'd done nothing this spontaneous or this daring before. He couldn't wait for this new experience.

******

Kate opened her hotel room door and breathed the crisp air. The horizon had a hint of sun. After her busy day yesterday driving around Napa Valley, she'd expected it would tire her this morning.

She'd visited several of the area's wineries, even contemplated going on the wine train, but ended up passing on the idea. Not sharing the ride with someone she knew hadn't felt right.

Her stomach churned with anticipation as she headed toward the outside stairs of the motel. From her window, she'd located the small gathering at the far corner of the hotel's parking lot where the balloon company's bus waited. The group traveling to the launch site would meet here.

She wore a lightweight jacket and patted the zippered pockets for her room key, the Jeep keys, her small billfold, and her cell phone. Yes, she had it all. See, Liz, your mother can operate on her own.

Yet, as she strode across the parking lot, she felt a twinge of loneliness. It struck her even more when she noticed all the pairings in the group. Two young couples, staring at each other, newlyweds. A family, complete with parents regarding their two elementary-aged children, a boy and a girl. Two middle-aged sisters, both checking cameras dangling around their necks. Four teenagers, friends. And a tall, bald man in khakis and a light jacket, glancing apprehensively around.

Because of all the other obvious pairings, she imagined that she and this man would get put together in one of the gondola's separated compartments. She could accept that and felt comfortable with the idea. They appeared to be of similar age.

So, why not introduce herself while they were waiting to load into the bus? She drew in a determined breath, squared her shoulders, and walked right over to him.

"Hi, I'm Kate, Kate Henderson." She gave him her best smile. "Is this your first balloon trip?"

******

Joe blinked in surprise at the woman in a bright pink windbreaker and jeans who had stopped in front of him and spoke cheerfully. Her short hair was reddish brown with lighter streaks often worn by younger women. Time had etched lines around her striking blue eyes and around her dimpled mouth. She wasn't as young as the others in the group, some place around his age. He relaxed, even returned her smile.

He thought about holding out his hand for a handshake but decided that was too formal. "Joe Thatcher," he said. "Yes, this is my first balloon trip. You?"

Excitement lit her expressive eyes. "I've wanted to do this my whole life. I decided it was now or never."

He watched the group progress toward the bus and nodded so she noticed. "Unlike you, I hadn't ever thought about doing this." He trailed behind her, almost feeling her eagerness. His initial interest had waned during the night until he'd almost changed his mind.

"My son thinks I'm crazy," he shared, without admitting that he'd wondered if it wasn't true. "Troy didn't come right out and say it but I understood what he thought."

She laughed, a soft sound that reminded him of his wife's gentle laugh. For a second, he missed sweet Charlotte. He would never forget her but he was plodding on with his life.

"My daughter wanted me to wait until we could go together." Kate glanced back at him while mounting the bus's steps.

"But you didn't want to wait, did you?" Somehow, he perceived this was a woman who tended not to over-think things and acted. Like his wife had done, much more than he'd been comfortable with. He'd learned to accept her determined independence, though, because he loved her.

"I couldn't see us finding a time to do it," she explained. "So, I came myself."

"Your husband not quite the adventurer you are?" He'd noticed her wedding band and wondered why she was here alone.

"He wasn't."

Joe realized that she was a widow or divorced. He suspected it was the prior. He decided not to pursue something so private and teased, "But you're a daredevil, aren't you?"

She laughed and slid into a seat at the back. "Not really." She paused. "Well, sometimes. I like to try new things." Like kayaking on the river with her sister's family. Like zip-lining in Maui.

When he sat beside her, she added, "I'm working my way through my bucket list. Things yet to do in my life."

For a second, his breath snagged on a memory. On their 25th anniversary, he and Charlotte had sat down—at her insistence—to make a long list of places they wanted to see, experiences they wanted to share. Driving a camper around the west, seeing Devil's Tower in Colorado and Mount Rushmore, and so much more. Most of which they hadn't accomplished. A sad truth he faced now.

Kate touched his arm, drawing his attention again. "Are you all right?"

He shook off the sorrow. "Sorry. I was just recalling what my wife and I had talked about doing."

"Widowed?" Her thoughtful eyes mirrored sympathy.

He nodded.

"It's painful." She didn't wait for him to respond. "I have lots of regrets about what my husband and I missed doing." She pulled in a breath and smiled as she blew it out. "I have more wonderful memories than regrets. That's what I focus on."

"I try to." Every day got easier. Those memories more precious.

As the bus moved, she glanced out the window. "I'm making new memories."

That was what he was doing, too. Yes, he liked that idea. New memories, without forgetting the old ones.

******

"Oh, look at that!" Kate pointed with one hand toward the multi-colored, striped balloon closest to them midst a half dozen balloons. It narrowly missed striking a tree on the hill they were passing over. "I bet they could reach out and touch a tree."

Joe's gut told him that their pilot would get them up-close-and-personal to the hill, too. The notion made him edgy. A lot of the flight made him feel that way. Not that he would admit it to the woman who shared a portioned off spot in the basket with him. Her enthusiasm and pure delight had allayed his wariness.

Until now.

"Don't even think about it."

"Think about what?" Kate's eyes hinted at amusement when she peeked at him.

He might not know everything about her but he'd already discovered that she pushed the limits sometimes. He couldn't count the number of times he'd had to latch onto her before she leaned a little too far over the side of the gondola to take a picture with her cell phone.

"Touching a tree."

"Would I do that?" She giggled.

"In a heartbeat."

She chuckled and gazed over the side.

They were too close to the treetops. Joe was sure the brazen woman would try it. Just as the bottom of the basket scooted over some branches, he sensed her struggle with temptation. His heart raced with apprehension. Unable to stand it another second, he curled his arm around her waist and tugged her against him.

She gasped in surprise and then sassed, "Spoilsport."

But she didn't pull away, letting him hold on to her until they were safely away from the trees and back to sailing through the sky. Until he could breathe once more.

Something had changed between them during these short hours together. Joe didn't understand all but something had. They'd laughed from the beginning when she hadn't been able to climb into the basket by herself. It hadn't embarrassed her when he and the pilot had lifted her into it firemen-style. It would have mortified Charlotte but Kate just laughed it off. After that, they'd shared the beauty and wonder of flying over vineyard after vineyard.

"I'm good now," she said, drawing him from his reflections. "I promise not to do anything outrageous."

Amazed that he was still holding onto her, he released her. They separated as much as they could in their restricted space. Neither spoke again for the rest of the trip back to the landing site. She delighted in the whole landing process, taking picture after picture. He simply observed her.

After they landed, and the balloon company's staff helped the others out of the gondola, he waited for his turn. He missed being near the woman who had made him laugh today. He'd enjoyed their time together. The group would eat a special brunch together and that would end their day.

When his feet were on the ground again, he glanced around for her. Curious Kate stood next to their collapsing balloon, taking even more pictures. It made him smile.

"I didn't even take one picture." He stepped beside her. "I'm not much of a picture-taking guy, anyway." But he wished he had a few, for those new memories he'd made.

She continued snapping away. "Give me your email address and I'll send you some of mine."

"I'd like that." Joe pulled his phone out of his pocket, making a sudden decision. "How about taking a selfie together?" He'd never done one before. Today was a first for a lot of things.

******

"Dad, I thought you were coming back tonight?"

Joe looked across the table at Kate, only half-listening to his son. "Tomorrow, Troy. I'll be back sometime tomorrow."

Kate was going through her photos, oooing and ahhhing every few seconds. She had the prettiest smile.

"Where are you? What's that funny noise I hear?" Troy asked.

"I took a wine tour train ride." He grinned at the woman who'd changed his plans about returning tonight. All she'd said was, "Do you want to try another adventure?" He hadn't given it a second's thought before agreeing.

"With a new friend," he added.

"Friend? Dad—"

"Don't worry about it, son. I'll be home tomorrow." He disconnected and met Kate's amused gaze. "Kids. Think they need to know everything."

She laughed, her eyes bright in amusement. "The news stunned my daughter, too, when I called her." She shrugged. "They'll survive."

Joe didn't know where this would go with Kate. It didn't matter. For now, they were making new memories. And he was happier than he'd been in a long time.

LIFE'S TWISTS AND TURNS

She was at it again.

Jared Baker froze coffee cup in hand in the doorway to the patio. His new neighbor wearing a body-hugging leotard and tights was bending forward, eyes closed. She leaned over until her palms flattened on the rug covering her adjoining patio. He should go back in his apartment and give her some privacy. That was the right thing to do.

Yet he stood as if rooted to the spot. He watched, mesmerized, as she bent forward until her arms strained taking more and more of her weight. Slowly, she lifted one leg and then the other, moving until her knees rested above her elbows. He gaped in amazement. How could she do that? With his bad back, he had trouble just bending to reach his knees.

His pulse had stepped up a good twenty beats, more maybe. He told himself it wasn't because he appreciated his neighbor's slender, well-toned form. Heavens, he was a sixty-eight-year-old man. His days of… Well, they were long over with. No, his reaction was because of the shocking things she could do with her body.

"Good morning, Jared," Carolyn Tyler said, saving him from his ridiculous thoughts. She twisted her head to look his way. Her chin-length, white hair swinging with the movement around her face. She had to be around the upper sixties, like him. But she sure didn't look it.

"Uh…good morning." He tightened the hold on his cup and stepped outside.

She smiled, the faint lines around her mouth deepening. Her gaze seemed to slide over Jared from his sock-covered feet to his Bermuda shorts to his loose-fitting T-shirt. Self-conscious, he sucked in his gut and thrust his shoulders back. He hadn't realized how far out of condition he was until she studied him. He needed to spend a little more time at the gym. His occasional drop-in maybe once a month wasn't cutting it.

He decided not to think too hard along that line. "You do this every day?" Stupid question. He'd already witnessed her doing this nearly every morning since she'd moved into the active senior apartment complex almost a month ago.

An early riser, he walked out onto his patio just after dawn to savor his first cup of coffee now that it was spring. He'd sit in his cushioned rocker, sip the hot brew, and listen to the birds in the nearby trees. Retired and widowed, he had plenty of time for observing nature. Plenty of time for mulling over what he might or might not do that day. After maintaining a rigid schedule all his working years, his schedule had become lax.

But Carolyn had messed up those peaceful times. His old heart couldn't keep starting his days spying his neighbor in one eye-catching outfit after another, contorting her body in some bizarre way. She would drive him to an early grave.

"I like a little yoga first thing in the morning. It gets me ready for whatever comes along that day." She closed her eyes again.

She appeared at ease in that peculiar position. How could that be? Even just observing her, his arms ached in empathy with hers, felt strained from tightened muscles.

Scrutinizing her, he considered the other quirky things he'd discovered about the woman. With the nice weather, he often had his patio door open to let in a fresh breeze through the screen door. Her door was usually open, too. Many times, he'd heard her singing off-key along to show tunes from the past. It always made him smile. His wife also had had no musical talent. It had made her self-conscious and she'd rarely sang, not even in church. But lack of skill didn't bother Carolyn. She sang her heart out. In fact, she was humming now, which made him smile.

She appreciated all kinds of music. Often her radio played everything from the oldies-but-goodies to Elvis Presley, to Fats Domino, to Country. A few times he'd even heard that crazy hip-hop stuff and rap. Whatever she had on, it was loud. Maybe her hearing wasn't what it used to be, like his. More amused than annoyed he'd never complained.

He knew she danced in her apartment. He'd been standing out on his patio by the railing looking around when he'd glanced into her place by accident. As always, she'd cranked up the music and was twisting and grinning in pure bliss. A dance he'd never mastered. He was a terrible dancer, something his wife had teased him about.

Carolyn shifted again, snaring his attention. She lowered her feet to the rug once more. Then she walked her hands back and slid them up her lithe body until she was standing. "There," she said, sounding satisfied and not at all out of breath. "I feel so much better."

Jared couldn't imagine that. "Right. Better," he responded sounding doubtful. He expected to see her arms trembling after holding her weight for so long. And to see weariness on her face. Instead, she looked energized, like that crazy pink bunny in the ads.

Her brown eyes twinkled, and she zeroed in on his coffee cup. "Yoga is far better for you than a jolt of caffeine. Trust me."

"But I like that jolt. I like coffee," he grumbled. "Besides, I've heard that some medical professionals are saying it's good for you." Okay, his doctor wasn't one. The man had told Jared to cut back on the amount he drank daily. His compromise had been to invest in a Keurig coffee maker that brewed one cup at a time, instead of having a whole pot available all day long. He considered that a big change.

She rolled her eyes in disagreement. "Green tea would be healthier."

He wrinkled his nose in disgust. "That would be like drinking pond water. No thanks." He took another sip of coffee that had already cooled and held little appeal now. Because she was watching him with one of those tolerant looks women excelled at, he took one more sip. It was awful.

Her lips twitched but she didn't outright laugh at his stubborn act. She reached for a hand towel on the arm of a wicker chair next to her. Stupid as it was, he watched in fascination as she mopped at the faint sheen of sweat on her brow.

Jared shook off that reaction and went back to holding in his gut, doubting he was deceiving her. He didn't have a bulging beer belly or anything. Still… "I'm healthy enough."

She flashed him an accepting smile. He detected a slight gap in her front teeth. It was charming and he liked learning that she wasn't as near-perfect as he'd first thought.

"Have you ever tried yoga?" Her eyes twinkled.

"I exercise." He thrust out his chin. The words "liar, liar, pants on fire" played through his thoughts.

One of her eyebrows lifted. "Really? You belong to an exercise club?"

"Yes," he said, not wanting to be pressed about it. He tried to remember the last time he'd stepped into the YMCA where he could use his Silver Sneakers membership.

When his beloved Judy had been alive, she'd convinced him to sign up for a couple's membership to the YMCA. She'd gone on and on about the abundance of exercise equipment, about the pool for swimming laps, and about the many kinds of classes. He'd rarely gone. He'd told her he got enough exercise walking around in the classroom as he taught high school workshop classes. Plus, he helped with coaching boys' basketball. And there was the vast lawn he used to mow when they still had a house in the suburbs. He had none of that these days.

"Do you actually go there?"

Sometimes women just couldn't leave a subject alone. "I walk around the park several times a week," he hedged, feeling guilty at the same time. Okay, his outings had fallen back to maybe twice a week, sometimes once a week.

"Good for you." She dropped the towel. She raised her arms to shoulder level and did side-to-side twists. "At least that's something."

He watched, not the least bit tempted to do it himself. Carolyn's arms were slender, with a hint of the droopy wings many women griped about having as they aged. Not that he'd noticed, unless his wife had grumbled about it. And he'd tried to tell her it wasn't any big deal. He'd been better off keeping his mouth shut. That was true about voicing his opinion on a lot of women's personal things.

"I play golf," he continued, although he couldn't remember the last time he had. He wasn't even sure where his golf clubs were at the moment. In storage? At his son's house?

"My husband used to play." She did more twisting, smiling. "He never could persuade me to go with him. I didn't see much sense in hitting a small ball around like that." She paused for a second. "I used to play tennis in a women's league. When I was much younger."

He'd guessed that she was a widow, but he never knew quite what to say about that. "I've never played tennis." He thought about something he'd read in the last senior center newsletter. "It seems people are playing pickleball now. Maybe I should try that." Maybe. He wasn't sure he had that much energy these days.

"I've heard about it, too. Sounds interesting." She went back to twisting around. Her hair swept back and forth across her cheeks. He noticed a faint white scar on the side of her neck, wondered how she'd gotten it. But he wouldn't ask, too personal.

"Well, I think it's time I went inside." He gave her a look of challenge and held up his cup. "Coffee has grown cold. Time to fix a new cup."

She chuckled, her eyes bright in amusement. "Green tea would be better."

"Not happening." He turned to go back into his apartment, realizing he'd enjoyed their first real conversation. Maybe you could become friends, just friends. He had no lady friends, hadn't even thought about it before. But perhaps you should.

"You should come to the yoga class I teach at the senior center."

Her invitation caught him off-guard. He had visions of watching her contorting in all kinds of weird poses. Then he saw himself trying them and failing. Too tough on a man's ego.

"Thanks. I'll just keep walking in the park." Safer. Less embarrassing, too. Or he could go to the Y. He'd have to think about it.

"If you change your mind," she murmured, "you're always welcome."

******

Carolyn had just spread another large blue cushioned mat on the floor of the main exercise room when she heard footsteps in the doorway. Her regulars were arriving. She was always happy to see them, glad to visit with the dozen older women who came to her classes. A couple had already become good friends. This move from the town she and Edward had lived in their entire marriage had been a good one. She'd needed a fresh start after his death. And it was good being here around her son and his kids. Now she could go to their ballgames and school functions.

She listened to the sound of her students putting their purses and water bottles on the table along the wall. Several of them started conversations, one laughed at something someone had said. All of it made her smile as she turned to face them.

But it was the uncomfortable-looking man in black exercise shorts that hung to his knees and a loose-fitting black T-shirt that snagged her attention. She blinked in amazement. Jared Baker. It had been over a week since she'd talked to him on their adjoining patios. Not for a second had she thought he would show up at her class.

The other women were sizing him up, trying not to flat-out gawk at him. Only rarely did a man join their class of active seniors. The men who came to this center seemed to shy away from what they considered the female courses. They played pool or cards or hung out in the TV room. She knew how much gumption it had taken for Jared to come today… and to not turn around and run for his life. Although in another second without her intervention, he might do that.

She hustled toward him, smiling. "Decided to try it? I'm glad."

He appeared relieved that she'd come to his rescue. The tension in his jaw eased. His dark brown eyes didn't look so worried. "I came to try out pickle ball." He heaved a disgruntled breath. "Found out it doesn't start for another hour. So…"

He hadn't come in response to her invitation. Carolyn felt disappointed. Still, she had him here, and that was a huge step. Others in their apartment complex had commented a time or two that he was a nice man. They thought he was lonesome, but he kept to himself. And, yes, she'd also heard that quite a few of the widowed women had tried to entice him to join in their occasional social events. Some had even taken him casseroles or special desserts that might draw him out. It hadn't worked. She imagined that her dear husband would have reacted much the same way. Which made her recognize that she had a soft spot in her heart for Jared.

She stepped closer and took hold of his hand. He stiffened but didn't jerk free, which pleased her. Ignoring the questioning looks they were getting, she tugged him with her toward the nearest mat at the back of the room.

When she stopped and released him, she gave him a teasing smile. "Bet you thought I would lead you to a mat up front."

"Yep, I feared that." A hint of a smile lifted one corner of his mouth. "This will be much better for both of us."

She enjoyed the sound of his rich voice, the slight rumble to it. She also liked his trimmed band of white hair and his short beard. Her husband had gone bald early in their marriage but she'd never minded. Unlike Edward, who had been about her same height, Jared stood a good six inches taller than her. His shoulders were broad, his arms still toned. But he had a slight paunch. She smiled at remembering how he'd tried to hide it from her. Sucking in his gut, standing straighter. Silly man.

Her gaze veered to the wall clock and she made her way to the front of the room. The women had found their favorite spots, ready for the class to begin. Although she caught a few of them glancing back toward the rare man in their midst. While she had loved her husband for over forty years and was still adjusting to his loss, she couldn't deny that her new neighbor intrigued her. She cherished her close friends back home that she kept in touch with. And she had already made several new friends here. But she missed having a man around to talk with, to disagree with, to challenge. She wanted nothing more than that.

She glanced across the room, found Jared watching her. Their gazes met for just a second. Something connected between them, something she couldn't explain. But it filled her with peace.

She darted him a challenging look. "Let's take it to the mat, ladies... and gentleman. We'll start with the lotus pose."

As she sat down, knees out wide, she drew her heels close. Her students followed her demonstration as best they could. Even Jared made a valiant attempt, with a quiet groan. Still, he tried.

"Have I mentioned, everyone, how good green tea is for the body?" She couldn't resist looking at Jared again. Her lips twitched at the roll of his eyes. "Some say it tastes like..."

"Pond scum." His face reddened when the ladies glanced at him, a couple giggling.

She, too, laughed. "Perhaps we can have a private discussion on the matter sometime."

"Perhaps," he muttered, then concentrated on drawing his heels close to his body, grimacing from the effort.

Ah, a baby step. She found herself impatient to finish the class, restless to get home. She might just make him a big glass of green tea and get him to sit with her on their patios. They could talk about... Well, anything.

A SPECIAL NIGHT

Ted glanced with frustration out the picture window in the living room. Dark clouds skidded across the sky as they had done for most of the late January day. They had spit snow off and on, which had worried him. He and Marie should spend tonight inside where it was pleasant and warm. His seventy-five-year-old body wouldn't appreciate going out in this mess.

He nudged the disgruntled thought aside and yelled, "Are you coming, Marie? It's almost five o'clock." That wasn't late unless you settled in early for the evening most of the time.

"What's your hurry, old man?" his cherished wife called back, using the "endearment" she used when he tested her patience. He smirked at the notion. They'd tried each other's patience for a lot of years and he would like to do that for many more. Sadly, he didn't think that would happen.

Not wanting to even consider that depressing idea, he grumbled, "Just dab on your lipstick. Let's go." She'd be rolling her eyes at him for that, which made him smile again. How many times over the years had he seen her do that? Way more than he could count.

Any other night Ted would just as soon have stayed home, tucked into his well-worn recliner, TV tuned to whatever ballgame was on that day. But tonight was different. When Marie had gone next door to visit their neighbor earlier, he'd set the TV's recorder, and called Trombolli's Restaurant, the best Italian food in town. He'd even reserved one of their special corner tables and requested a bottle of their favorite wine be put aside for them. He was darn proud of himself for making all the plans. Mr. Romantic, he was not. Today he'd upped his game, as their grandson would say.

He glanced at the watch she'd given him for their twenty-fifth anniversary. He'd given her a new toaster. Their daughter had huffed in disgust. He'd impressed his son-in-law and son with his practicality. Marie had laughed until she cried.

Pushing back the memory, he called out, "Marie, get a move on!" Patience. After all these years, he knew a man had to have patience with a woman. She was pushing his limit though.

She stepped into the living room doorway. "What's up with you?" Her expression mirrored confusion. "Normally, I have to drag you kicking and screaming out after three in the afternoon."

"What's hard to understand? I said we're going out tonight and we are."

Ted saw the impulse to question him more flitting across her time-wrinkled face. He could look at that face any time of any day. He didn't even notice the wrinkles she sometimes fretted about. All he saw was the woman he'd married fifty years ago, the one who still took his breath away.

"Get your coat and hat, honey. It's cold out."

"Maybe we should stay in if it's so cold." She glanced past him to see the weather outside and shivered.

His old bones would have preferred staying home but he wasn't sure how many more chances they'd have for a night like this. Besides, this was special. "Not tonight," he insisted.

She still looked unsure but smiled in acceptance. With her usual grace, she moved to the thick-cushioned sofa they'd bought last year to replace the one that had worn out. He'd placed the black leather coat with the big fur collar she loved so much over the arm.

He missed her challenging him over every little thing. Her spirited Italian temper had mellowed over the years, more so this last year. Her health had gone downhill, his, too. It seemed with every doctor appointment they both got more prescriptions. Since she'd begun forgetting more things, her doctor had suggested that he manage their pill boxes. His heart ached realizing they might not have a lot of time left together.

Ted blinked away the tears burning his eyes. He'd had moments when he allowed himself to cry in private about the situation. He could never let her see him like that.

He cleared his throat, so she wouldn't suspect he was feeling emotional. "Here, let me help you, Sweet Marie," he suggested, using his familiar pet name.

Independent woman that she still was, she waved him off. "I can put a coat on by myself, thank you very much. Leave me be, you old fool." She struggled into the coat, regarding him with filmy eyes burdened with cataracts.

He forced himself to keep his distance. She needed this independence more than she required his help. All too soon that would change. Again, he fought back tears that threatened to spill out. Old fool is right. He didn't want to think about any of that getting-older business tonight.

As she reached for the strange knitted hat she'd made years ago—a hat he thought pitiful looking, he pulled on his own fading leather coat. She tugged the multi-colored hat down over her ears. It made her reddish-blondish-whitish hair flip up all around the lower edge of the hat. He planted the plaid wool cabby-style hat she'd given him for his fortieth birthday on his balding head. He guessed his hat was in as sorry a shape as hers but he wouldn't give it up, either.

"Okay, I'm ready," she said at last, all bundled up. Her brow furrowed. "Where did you say we're going?"

"I didn't say and you know it. This is a surprise." Even if he'd told her earlier, she probably wouldn't have remembered.

He glanced down and noted that she still had on her house slippers. She'd forgotten about them again. That pinch of pain around his heart squeezed harder.

"Just a minute." He scurried off to the bedroom for her dress shoes. This was better. If he mentioned the problem, she would get embarrassed. He didn't want that.

When he returned with the shoes, she smiled as if what he'd done was normal. She let him exchange her slippers for the sturdy shoes, not even questioning why he did it. Just accepted what he was doing and held out one small foot after the other.

He stood, his ancient bones creaking from having bent over. Swallowing back a lump in his throat, he took Marie's slight hand and led her out of the house. He tried not to think about how frail that hand was, how paper-thin the skin, skin that bruised so easily these days. His own hands were getting that way, too. Except his hands were much bigger.

With a hand to her back, he urged her out the laundry room door into the garage. When she was settled in the passenger seat, she gazed up at him. "Are we going to Patricia's? We haven't seen the grandkids in ages. I've missed seeing them."

That pinch around his heart returned. Every day was getting harder.

He hesitated to answer. They'd seen their daughter and her kids just last weekend. Last week, today, tomorrow, ten years ago. Time didn't matter in Marie's world anymore.

With a forlorn sigh, he told her where they were going. "Not to Patricia's. I'm taking you to Trombolli's."

A crease eased between her thin white eyebrows, then she nodded but looked worried.

He walked with a heavy step around to the driver's side of the 20-year-old Chevy Impala he wouldn't trade for any fancy new car. Like his precious wife, it was a keeper.

When he eased onto the driver's seat, Marie glanced at him with uncertainty. "Today is special, isn't it?" She worried her lower lip and focused on her age-spotted hands curled in her lap. "I should know, shouldn't I?" she asked in a sad whisper.

Fifty years today. Yes, Marie should know what today meant. Birthdays and anniversaries had once meant so much to her. Now they were just a blur. She used to keep meticulous notes on the calendars always on the front of their refrigerator. But not this year. They hadn't even put up a calendar. She hadn't even noticed. And he hadn't had the courage to mention it.

He gulped down that irritating lump in his throat again. "It's a special night because I'm taking my Sweet Marie out to her favorite restaurant, that's all." Never would he tell her the truth. It would make her sad that she didn't remember. He wanted her as happy as possible for whatever time she had left with him.

"Oh, it's too expensive." She frowned at him. In that moment in time, she seemed to remember how much of a penny-pincher he'd been during their years together. "We should stay home. I can make us dinner."

He was not pinching pennies tonight. He reached over to stop any further protest by putting a finger to her thin lips. "Nothing's too expensive for my wife." Those stupid tears stung his eyes again, but he ignored them. "Now, buckle up. We're going out to eat and that's that."

Before he could pull his finger away, she caught his hand, turned it, and kissed his shaking hand. "You're a good husband, Ted, and I love you so much."

He would treasure those words forever, hold them close as they struggled together through whatever came next. She was his life.

"Not half as much as I love you, old woman," he croaked. "Enough of this sappy stuff. We need to get going." He smiled at her, memorized every beautiful thing about her again.

"Remember the first time we went to Trombolli's?" She sounded lost in her memories, not expecting an answer. "We shared lasagna and garlic bread. Had our first wine that night."

He'd eaten far too much of the garlic bread, the best he'd ever tasted. Smiling as he backed out of the garage, he shared his own memory. "You wouldn't let me kiss you. Said I had garlic breath."

She giggled, coming back to the moment. "Remember that tonight. No kisses for you later if you pig out on the garlic bread."

"I won't even have one piece." He reached over to squeeze her leg. "I'd rather have your kisses than anything else."

Her face looked younger in that instant, at least to him. Her eyes sparkled with life once more. That cute dimple he'd always liked appeared. "Such a flirt you are," she said in that teasing way he hadn't heard in far too long. "You might just get lucky tonight."

He'd been blessedly lucky for these last fifty years. He wanted fifty more.

YESTERDAY, TODAY, TOMORROW

"The kids will be here in a week," Robert said, walking up behind Peggy. "Are you going to have this project finished?"

Peggy leaned back in her chair at the dining room table. Her back ached and her eyes burned. "What did you ask?" She hadn't been listening to him.

He blew out a breath. "I asked if you will get this project finished in time."

She'd been sitting here for several hours but had made little progress on the scrapbook for her daughter. So far, all she'd managed was to bury the table with old photographs, school papers, award ribbons, and lots of memorabilia. She was a "keeper" of items many people tossed out. Her storage closet boasted boxes and plastic tubs filled with memory items from years past. There were boxes of things that defined her history, her husband's life, lives of various family members outside their own small family unit, and of her daughter's life. It was too much stuff to sort through and make sense of unless you were determined.

"I'll have it done." She heard the stress echoing in her voice. She would have this project completed before her daughter and son-in-law arrived for Christmas. Even if she had to work 24/7 until then. "Why did I procrastinate on this so long?"

He reached down to massage her tense shoulders, making her groan in appreciation. "Beats me. Usually when you decide to do something, you get right on it."

That was true. She threw herself into whatever project of the moment had her attention. Except this one. This was a project she'd been talking about for several years and had finally decided this would be the year she finished it. Not that her daughter knew about it. Peggy wanted to surprise her and her new husband. She looked forward to watching them sit together and go through the "Book of Callie's Life," pre-Eric.

"Maybe you could help me." She glanced up at her husband of forty-four years.

He lifted an eyebrow, his grin crooked before he shook his head. "Not my thing."

No kind of craft project interested him. He supported whatever she liked but helping her wasn't something he ever volunteered to do. "Fine. Then you can at least supply me with nourishment while I plow through all of this." She waved a hand at the chaos spread on the table. "I'm starving."

"That I can do. How about beef stroganoff?" He headed for the kitchen, agreeable to making the best of his limited cooking dishes.

"Sounds good." Peggy went back to searching over the years of memories in front of her. With a sigh, she reached for the stack of photos. She needed to separate them by age and choose which ones to include in the scrapbook. She would keep them all. But only a specific selection would go into the book of her daughter's history.

******

Robert observed his wife dab at a tear slipping down her cheek then sniff. This same thing had happened over and over the last couple of days. The scrapbook project played with her heartstrings. He couldn't count the number of times she'd called out to him to come see another souvenir or photograph that had stopped her progress. She insisted that he relive each photographic moment. Or remember when their daughter had received a particular school award. Or...

Well, every item she picked up brought back memories to her. But he had to admit he didn't remember a lot of them, not that he would ever admit that to Peggy.

Again, she had sat at that table for long hours today. She needed a break. He needed a break. He climbed out of his recliner. "How about we go to the mall? Walk around a little, get some exercise." This was a significant offer on his part since he detested going to the mall, considered it walking through a man's version of Hell.

She peered up from a crayon drawing their daughter had done to look at him. "I'm only making a little progress on this project. I don't think—"

"Honey, you've been thinking too much." He held her gaze. "Some time away from whatever you're doing will do you good." Him, too. Today she focused on sorting through Callie's early schoolwork. She intended to make sense of the many crayon drawings she had kept, and far too often asking him about them. Most of the time he didn't have a clue what they were. Callie's early work had been abstract, to say the least.

Peggy set down the piece of construction paper with some wild attempt of Callie's at drawing her family. "I guess you're right. My backside is hurting from sitting here so long." She brightened, her eyes sparkling, and he sensed danger. "Besides, we need to pick up a couple more gifts. Small stuff. Stocking stuffers."

With a groan, Robert headed for the entry closet and snagged their coats. "Sure. Shopping. You know I live for it," he mumbled. What had he been thinking to suggest this outing?

She laughed, got up with a moan. "You asked for this."

He had. "Will you have pity on me? Make me suffer through shopping for only a short time? Say maybe a half hour."

"Right!" She chortled and walked over to let him help her with her coat.

******

Her husband was withering, his steps becoming slower and slower. But he hadn't complained. Yet. Peggy expected that would soon change. She started to tell him they could leave the mall now but a quirky dish towel with a pair of flamingos in Hawaiian outfits snagged her attention in a nearby store. She bee-lined for the rack of towels just inside the kitchen store.

Robert heaved a sigh behind her as he followed. "I thought we were done." He sounded like a petulant child.

"This will be the last gift. I promise." She drew the linen towel from the rack. "You've been a real trooper. Thank you."

He was already pulling out his billfold and heading for the checkout counter. "Just glad to see you not so stressed. That project was getting to you."

It had been, and she was a long way from finished. "I'll try not to get so engrossed with every school paper. I need to quit going back in mental time to when Callie brought them home. I need to decide what goes in the scrapbook. And what goes back in the memory boxes."

As they left the store and headed toward the mall exit, he juggled the bags he carried. He caught her hand, slid their fingers together, and squeezed them. "I'm proud of you, honey. For having bothered to keep all of that stuff. For wanting to make something special for our daughter."

She paused on the sidewalk and looked up at the man she'd married what felt like just yesterday. They'd both changed. He had quit playing softball years ago. Yet in her mind's eye she could still see the athlete he'd been. His long, toned legs running from base to base. His snagging a ball in his mitt as a shortstop. She still had his well-worn mitt, even a couple of his old uniform shirts. Someday she planned to make a T-shirt quilt with his old ball team uniforms and their daughter's. Someday. Her to-do list was mind-boggling.

"What? Is something wrong?" he asked, his tone worried. His forehead creased.

Peggy smiled, coming back to the moment. "Everything is perfect. I was just thinking, remembering." Ahead of them, snowflakes fell and she laughed. "Look! It's snowing!"

After a final concerned glance at her, he tugged her across the parking lot. "We'd better get going before I have to clean off the car. I hope we don't have to scrape windows."

She dashed with him and her thoughts traveled to another time in bad weather with him and their daughter. When she pulled open her car door, she looked across the roof at him. "Remember that time when Callie cleaned off the windshield in the parking lot? When she stepped back from the car and you drove away, forgetting she was still outside?"

Robert groaned and gave her a glower, but amusement lingered in his blue eyes. "Something I will never live down."

"No." She laughed and slid into the car. "Just another memory to treasure." There were so many of them. She liked to pull them out from time to time, savor them.

"Okay. I'm ready to head home and get back to my project. I think I know where I'm going with it now. This time away helped."

She was also ready to finish it, so she could move onto other scrapbooks she wanted to create. One for her younger days. One for Robert's. One for their family vacations. And one for the many years of their marriage.

As her husband set their shopping bags in the backseat, she considered those upcoming projects. She needed to start one, too, for what would happen in their life ahead. These special books would become their memories of yesterday, today, and tomorrow.

"Maybe I can help you." Robert sat down and gave her a cautious glance. "Don't expect too much from me. But I'll help."

Be still my heart! "I'll take whatever help you can give me." She reached over to squeeze his leg. "I love you. Always have, always will."

It only took him a second before he said, "Love you, too." He turned on the engine and looked around before backing out of the parking space. "I think I fell in love with you when you introduced me to your parents by the wrong name. Stupid, I know."

She chuckled. "And that's something I will never live down." Another memory item to jot down in the scrapbook she'd create about their life together.

Life's Twists and Turns